ADRIFT IN CURRENTS CLEAN AND CLEAR

BY THE SAME AUTHOR

Deadlands: Boneyard
Dusk or Dark or Dawn or Day
Dying with Her Cheer Pants On
Laughter at the Academy
Letters to the Pumpkin King
Overwatch: Declassified:
An Official History of Overwatch
The Proper Thing and Other Stories

THE ALCHEMICAL JOURNEYS SERIES
Middlegame
Seasonal Fears
Tidal Creatures

THE WAYWARD CHILDREN SERIES
Every Heart a Doorway
Down Among the Sticks and Bones
Beneath the Sugar Sky
In an Absent Dream
Come Tumbling Down
Across the Green Grass Fields
Where the Drowned Girls Go
Lost in the Moment and Found
Mislaid in Parts Half-Known

Seanan McGuire's Wayward
Children, Volumes 1–3 (boxed set)
Be Sure: Wayward Children,
Books 1–3

THE OCTOBER DAYE SERIES
Rosemary and Rue
A Local Habitation
An Artificial Night
Late Eclipses
One Salt Sea
Ashes of Honor
Chimes at Midnight
The Winter Long
A Red-Rose Chain
Once Broken Faith
The Brightest Fell
Night and Silence
The Unkindest Tide
A Killing Frost
When Sorrows Come
Be the Serpent
Sleep No More
The Innocent Sleep

THE INCRYPTID SERIES
Discount Armageddon
Midnight Blue-Light Special
Half-Off Ragnarok
Pocket Apocalypse
Chaos Choreography
Magic for Nothing
Tricks for Free

ADRIFT IN CURRENTS CLEAN AND CLEAR

SEANAN McGUIRE

TOR PUBLISHING GROUP

NEW YORK

ADRIFT IN CURRENTS CLEAN AND CLEAR

Copyright © 2024 by Seanan McGuire

Interior illustrations by Rovina Cai

A Tordotcom Book
Published by Tom Doherty Associates / Tor Publishing Group
120 Broadway
New York, NY 10271

www.torpublishinggroup.com

Tor® is a registered trademark of Macmillan Publishing Group, LLC.

Library of Congress Cataloging-in-Publication Data

Names: McGuire, Seanan, author.
Title: Adrift in currents clean and clear / Seanan McGuire.
Description: First edition. | New York : Tor Dot Com,
Tor Publishing Group, 2024. | Series: Wayward children ; 10
Identifiers: LCCN 2024024442 | ISBN 9781250848338 (hardcover) |
ISBN 9781250848345 (ebook)
Subjects: LCGFT: Fantasy fiction. | Novels.
Classification: LCC PS3607.R36395 A66 2024 |
DDC 813/.6--dc23/eng/20240621
LC record available at https://lccn.loc.gov/2024024442

Our books may be purchased in bulk for promotional,
educational, or business use. Please contact your local bookseller
or the Macmillan Corporate and Premium Sales Department
at 1-800-221-7945, extension 5442, or by email at
MacmillanSpecialMarkets@macmillan.com.

First Edition: 2025

Printed in the United States of America

0 9 8 7 6 5 4 3 2 1

FOR CATHERYNNE, AND FOR NAOMI.
YOU HAVE BOTH LED ME THROUGH FORESTS.
NOW LET ME GUIDE YOU HERE.

Sing to me a river song, wide and swift and running:
Sing to me of river fish, silver-bright and cunning.
Sing to me an ocean song, deep and wide and true.
Sing to me of ocean fish, and they will sing of you.

—traditional greeting song, Belyyreka

She had spent a lifetime in Belyyreka, and they had always called her a Drowned Girl, even when she was away from the water, and she had never considered how literal that might be, not until she had fallen into a river and felt hands yanking her by the shoulders, away from the surface, away from the real world, back into the false one, where mothers left her, one after the other, where nothing ever stayed.

—*Beneath the Sugar Sky*

PART I

ON DRY LAND

1 NOT EVERYTHING IS MADE THE SAME

NADYA SOKOLOV, AS SHE grew older, would come to say that she had three mothers: the one who bore her, the country that poisoned her, and the one who adopted her. But when her story began, she knew no mother at all. She was born to an unmarried teenager in a state-run hospital, a girl whose own story has as yet gone unwritten, who pushed her firstborn daughter screaming and bloody into the world, already half-determined to run and leave the child behind, even before she got her first look at the baby.

As red and angry as any newborn, the not-yet-named Nadya shook her tiny fist in the air, and waved the unfinished stump of her right arm at the same time, making her fury and frustration clear. The girl who had never quite managed to think of herself as a mother, who never managed to imagine any involvement with her own child past this moment, looked at her and recoiled.

"Where is the rest of her?" she demanded of the nurse. "Is it still— Oh, God, is it still inside me?" Images of a baby's arm permanently wedged in her womb danced through her pain-mazed mind, more horrifying than even the baby's existence, which was horrific enough.

She had never asked for this. Not the pregnancy, not the prettiness which had made the pregnancy all but inevitable, not the boys who had danced attendance on her until the wages of their communal sins had begun to show—and hadn't the boys disappeared quickly after that? As if a girl could get herself pregnant without assistance, as if the boy who had been so quick to call himself a man while seeking her favor had no part in it at all! And most of all, she never asked for the child. God above, not the child.

And now the child is flawed, incomplete, and she can't do this. She was never meant to be a mother, or at least not *yet*, not *now*, not until she's more than a child herself. Not until she's had time to play.

The nurse, either unaware of or ignoring her patient's growing distress, shook her head and laughed, the deep, hearty laugh of a woman who'd seen more new mothers than she cared to remember. All of them were the same in this moment, sweaty and exhausted and worn thin, but aching for their babes. "No, no, her arm isn't inside you. Her arm never grew at all. See how smooth and rounded the skin is? That means there was nothing there to be torn away. This is how she was made. She's perfect as she is." She scooped the baby out of the warmer where she had been placed for cleaning and offered her to the frightened teen whose heartbeat the baby's body knew better than its own. "You can hold her if you'd like."

"No!" blurted the girl. Still torn open, bloody and bleeding and in an immeasurable amount of pain, she rolled away from the nurse and infant, almost toppling off the narrow birthing bed. At the last second she caught herself and wobbled in place, not falling to the floor. Pushing herself into a sitting position, she swung her legs around and stood, lurching for the door.

The nurses who had overseen the birth watched this with silent interest and, in some cases, amusement. This wasn't the first time many of them had seen an unmarried girl flee rather than face the consequences of her actions, even when those consequences had healthy lungs and all the parts that truly mattered. An arm? A hand? Pah! What was a hand? One was enough to let the girl bathe and dress herself, and work when the time came. Two hands were a luxury, and not necessary for a child who had no reason to aspire to great things.

The girl reached the door and staggered out of the room, leaving a trail of blood behind, never once looking back. The head nurse sighed and looked down at the child.

"She'll have the paperwork completed to leave you here and be gone before we finish cleaning you, if I read her right, little songbird," she said, a hint of regret in her voice. "And I do read her right, I've been doing this for thirty years and I've never guessed wrong."

"Do you want me to go after her, ma'am?" asked one of the junior nurses anxiously.

"And do what? Turn her into a different person altogether? Not enough magic left in all of Russia for that. The law says she can surrender her baby, and if that's what she desires to do, that's what will be done. As for this little songbird, we'll get her cleaned up, wait to see if the mother returns, and surrender her to the home if not."

"I see," said the junior nurse, somewhat disapproving.

The head nurse made silent note of her tone. They'd be discussing that later. For the moment, she had to focus on the baby, and so she carried her back to the warming box, humming an old song her grandmother used to sing to her, about the river that ran from one end of the world to the other, never stopping, never slowing.

By the time she put the baby down, the girl was staring at her with wide, fascinated blue eyes. The head nurse smiled.

"You understand nothing, little songbird, but even a stone can comprehend kindness. You'll have time enough to learn, I promise you."

THE GIRL, WHO HAD NEVER given her name or named her daughter, did not return, and so the baby was surrendered to the nearest orphanage, a state-run institution for wards of Mother Russia. She was not the only infant with a visible deformity, nor the worst-off of the new arrivals; having never possessed a right hand, she didn't miss it, and did perfectly well with her left, navigating and manipulating her world as adroitly as any other child. If certain tasks would always be more difficult for her, well, wasn't that true of everyone? No single person could do absolutely everything without aid, and so her own limitations weren't limitations at all, merely different standards.

They named her Nadezhda, a good, traditional name with plenty of room for her to grow into it, and they called her Nadya, and she was a good, sweet child who grew swift and straight as a reed, strong of back and swift of eye and quick to help the other children with their tasks, seeming to see without being informed how they could turn their collective weaknesses into strengths, all by combining them into a united front.

On the rare occasions when prospective parents came sniffing around the home for adorable new additions to their family, it was Nadya who organized the swarm into orderly ranks, highlighting whichever of her many brothers and sisters she had decided would most benefit from a home of their own, someplace less regimented and institutional. She had such a gift for it that the orphanage staff mostly just stood back in polite bemusement and allowed Nadya to work, not sure whether their presence would help or hinder her machinations.

"It's as if she has no interest in a family of her own," said one of the matrons, on the occasion of one such presentation to potential parents. "See how she never puts herself where they can properly see her? She'll age out if she's not careful."

"She's six, she's in no danger of aging out," said another of the matrons, taking pity. "And we've filled her head with stories of Mother Russia. She believes she already *has* a family. Her country is mother enough, and all the other orphans are her brothers and sisters. She wants what's best for her family, and that's why the children who want to leave us are always front and center when she arranges these little displays." Her tone turned fond. "Again, she's only six. She's going to be a terror when she's grown."

Nadya smiled and dimpled at the prospective parents, gesturing as much as possible with the stump of her right arm, making sure none of them could miss the fact that she was missing what too many of them would see as something crucial, rather than something she had never truly missed. The other children were styled to minimize any attributes that might have made it harder for them to find homes, while she was styled to accentuate hers.

That would, three years later, prove to be her downfall, but she was very far, as yet, from knowing that. She was young and sweet and innocent and hard, in the way of children raised in job lots rather than individually; she was doing her best to be a good person, and to figure out what that meant in the context of the world she knew and had and understood.

She liked the matrons, or most of them, at least; the younger ones were kinder, more inclined to play, more willing to answer her endless stream of questions. The older matrons had been worn down more by the system they belonged to, and found Nadya's endless optimism frustrating. Almost as frustrating as her tendency to wallow in the shallow river behind the orphanage, which was filthy and polluted but called to her in some way they couldn't understand or stop.

She had come in one day from the field between the orphanage and the river, holding a sickly tortoise under her arm, declaring loudly that his name was Maksim and she was going to make him healthy again. The orphanage didn't allow pets, of course, but a tortoise was quiet and made no unpleasant smells or messes; the matrons agreed, collectively, to turn the other way and pretend they didn't see the reptile, who was sure to die soon anyway.

But he didn't. Nadya brought him greens from the yard and cabbage and salad from her own plate; she cajoled the other children into letting her raid their leftovers, sparse as they were, for tidbits her tortoise might enjoy; and she guided him, one awkward, almost-accidental step at a time, back toward a healthy tortoise life. His scales brightened. His movements became quicker. His shell, which had been flaky and dull when she brought him inside, gleamed. He began to rove the orphanage halls with greater and greater frequency, until the matrons became hard-pressed to keep up the pretense that they didn't know he was there.

The next time potential parents came to visit, Nadya found a way to turn the conversation, even as she was introducing her available brothers and sisters, toward the brilliance of tortoises as beloved household companions. By late afternoon, as two of the younger children were on their way to a new life and new adventures, with the new parents to match, the newly minted father was cradling a tortoise under his arm, trying bemusedly to understand what had just happened.

But that was what it was like to run afoul of Nadya when she wanted something to happen. As for Nadya herself, she went back to the room she shared with almost a dozen other girls, and looked at the empty bowl next to her bed where she had always placed Maksim's ration of salad. She had done a good thing, the *right* thing, she knew she had. She always did the good thing, the right thing, and if she kept doing the good and right thing, maybe one day the mother who had fled from her would realize she had made a mistake and come back to claim her. She would hear it in the river, or carried on the wind; Russia herself would see what a good, biddable, obedient girl Nadya was, and tell her mother to come collect her.

Someday.

Nadya lay down on her bed, and pressed her face into her thin pillow, and cried.

Years slipped by, one after another, like leaves floating down the river, until Nadya was nine years old. She was quick and articulate, frequently bored in her classes, always willing to assist with chores, even beyond the ones she was assigned, and still she presented the other children and still she downplayed herself, until the day the missionary trip arrived in the office.

They were healthy and bright-eyed, these Americans, with sleek, shining hair and clear skin, dressed plainly in black and white, each with a name tag written in incomprehensible English lettering. Their paperwork was impeccable. They had managed, through bribery, careful applications, and understanding of the administrative systems they were dealing with, to circumvent the laws forbidding adoption of Russian children by foreign nationals. It was a mission of mercy, they said; they were there to help the most underprivileged children they could find, the ones with nowhere else to go.

The matrons bristled at this description of their charges, which dismissed all the work they'd done and all the care they'd given, but they wanted these children to have homes before they got too old and were pushed out the door to make room for the bodies who were always crowding behind them, hungry and in need of a place to call their own. They smiled stiffly and agreed to arrange for a viewing.

It began like any other. The matrons prepared the children according to the proper standards, while Nadya came through with standards of her own, tweaking and adjusting and preparing her brothers and sisters to put their best feet forward. When she moved to hang back as she always did, the matrons swept in and forced her into her own nicest dress, the one with the sleeve that hung down to what should have been wrist-length on her right side, making it harder to see her arm. She fussed and whined, but they pinned her in place and combed her hair.

"You can't stay here forever, Nadya," they scolded. "The years go by, and you remain. It's not right! A girl like you should have a home of her own, a family to prepare you to become a woman! You will be presented to them like a proper child, not as if you were a mascot meant to make the other children look more pleasant to potential parents. You are not a wild thing. Be a credit to those who have raised you."

At that, Nadya settled and allowed herself to be prepared. She was *not* a wild thing, but there was no way these parents from a foreign land would look at her and see their heart's desire. She had been marked by Mother Russia before she was born. It was there she would remain.

The children were ushered into the greeting room and pinned down by the bright eyes of the American missionaries, who seemed to home in on every tiny flaw. They dismissed perfect child after perfect child, spending their focus like precious coin on the ones who had been left there by parents afraid to love a baby with pieces missing, as if blindness or deafness or a foreshortened limb could somehow become contagious. Nadya almost managed to avoid their attention, thanks to the dress she had been given, until one of the matrons realized what was happening and called, in a trilling tone quite unlike her usual harsh orders:

"Oh, Nadezhda, darling, you forgot to pin up your sleeve!" She rushed in with a safety pin, folding up the tangling tube of fabric and pinning it securely in place while Nadya glared at her. She met the girl's glare with a smile, which only grew as the missionaries swarmed around her, this polite, well-mannered little girl who they had previously dismissed as not what they were looking for.

Three children left the orphanage that day. Gregor, who could not hear; Maria, with her seizures and sloping spine; and Nadya, whom they had taken for polite, biddable, and tame. She looked back over her shoulder as she was led away, carried into a new life she had never asked for or expected.

Her third mother had arrived at last, and Nadya was finally gone.

2 ALL-AMERICAN GIRL

NADYA'S ADOPTIVE PARENTS lived in a place called Denver, which was very tall and very dry. The air was thinner than she was accustomed to, and for the first week after they arrived, she was sick almost every day, with a pounding headache that refused to go away. They spoke loudly and quickly in English, which she had very few words of—and they had fewer of Russian— and she began to despair for ever being happy again. The matrons had given her to these people, who had bundled her onto an airplane and carried her halfway around the world, only to rush her into a doctor's office for a series of painful injections! And now this headache, which would not go away . . .

If they hadn't been feeding her, she would have thought they were trying to kill her. Since they *were* feeding her, and she was vomiting after almost every meal, it was still possible they were trying to kill her and were simply rich enough to be willing to waste food in the process. With no way to communicate and no strength to run away, it was impossible for her to tell.

On the morning of the sixth day, the man who wanted to be called "Daddy" came to sit on the edge of her bed and stroke her hair while she drank a glass of something sweet and fruity. "You need the electrolytes," he said, words incomprehensible to her, and smiled encouragingly when she swallowed the last sip. Then he tapped his forehead and asked, in an exaggeratedly slow voice, "Feeling better? Okay?"

"Okay" was one of the words she knew. "Okay" meant agreement, meant going along with whatever she was being asked. It also meant "yes," in a way she was still trying to understand.

Her head *did* feel somewhat better, and so she nodded, lowering the glass, and said, "Da. Okay."

He smiled and took the glass away from her, setting it on the bedside table, before offering his own hand in exchange. "Come with me. I want to show you something."

It was so much mild gibberish, but the intent was clear, and Nadya knew enough about adults to understand that biddability was sometimes the only thing that made them relax around you. If she ever wanted to get out of here and back to the orphanage—and after the length of the flight to get here, she knew it must be *hours* away on foot—she needed them to trust her, to think she was the kind of girl who would agree to things and not break any rules.

She nodded again, ignoring the way it sent pain shooting through her temples, and slipped her hand into his. "Da," she said. "Okay."

He beamed like he'd just won a prize as he led her out of the room they had prepared for her use, pink walls and pink furnishings and plush pink carpet—her new parents might have claimed not to have any preconceptions about the child they'd be bringing home from Russia, but they had clearly been expecting a girl—and into the browner, more neutral hallway. A fresh pair of shoes waited for her by the door, just her size, as pink as the curtains.

They felt like pillows on her feet. Nadya stared at them, wide-eyed, and tried a few experimental jumps, laughing a little when the pillowy texture remained intact. She turned up to "Daddy," beaming, and informed him in a cheery voice that the shoes were amazing, astonishing, the best she'd ever felt.

Her vocabulary went far beyond his limited Russian. Still, he could tell a happy child when he saw one, so he smiled indulgently back and said, "Yes, princess, they're all yours. Nice new shoes. Now let's just get your coat on and we can go."

None of her things from the orphanage had come with her to America; the coat he helped her into was also new, a rough blue velvety fabric that made little swishing noises when she rubbed her fingers over it. It fit her well, and she liked the feeling of the fabric, although it made her oddly sad for her old coat, which had been left behind. It had still been perfectly good for another year or two of wear, and if it had stopped fitting her before it came apart, it would have been handed down to one of the younger children.

She stiffened as she realized that it probably had been, by now. They'd have redistributed all her meager things, to make sure nothing was wasted, and the other children would remember her for a time, but eventually she'd be forgotten, as all the orphans who came before her had been. Who would remember Maksim? Who would treasure the happy little wiggle he gave when slipped a rare slice of fruit, and the funny bump on the edge of his shell?

He had been an orphan too. He deserved to be remembered. But she wasn't sure even the matrons would.

Her new father took her by the hand and led her out the door, into a bright new world where the sun was too bright and the air was sharp and dry, burning the back of her throat. She breathed in sharply and began to cough, causing him to look at her in momentary concern before he softened and nodded.

"The air here can take some getting used to, princess, but

you'll adjust, I promise. Come on." Still holding her hand, he began to walk.

Nadya buried her face against her sleeve to cover her coughing as she let herself be led, and bit by bit, it became easier for her to breathe. Bit by bit, the air stopped stinging quite so much, and she started to relax and look at her surroundings.

Everything here was so large and so *bright*. She had never seen anything like it in or around the orphanage. Cars zipped by on the street, but she paid them little mind; cars were, after all, familiar things, best avoided or ignored. As long as she didn't get into their way, it wasn't like they were going to leap up onto the walkway to get her.

Then they left the walkway for a narrow dirt path winding through a green space, peppered with unfamiliar trees. She looked up at the man and asked a question, and he smiled down at her.

"The nice ladies at the orphanage said you'd had a turtle once, and you missed him very much after he went away. So I thought you might want to come and see some turtles here."

None of that makes any sense, but Nadya nodded all the same. Better not to antagonize him as he led her deeper and deeper into the tall grass and the trees.

Then the path broadened out, and Nadya gasped.

The pond was small and almost perfectly spherical, with a low split-rail fence around it and several dead trees protruding from the dark water, their trunks mottled with rot and lichen. Turtles—unfamiliar turtles, but turtles all the same—lounged on the dead trees, heads extended to catch the sun.

"Cherepakha!" Nadya informed the man excitedly. "Cherepakha, cherepakha!"

That wasn't one of the words he knew, but given the context and what he'd been told at the orphanage, it wasn't hard for him to understand. He let go of her hand, gesturing for her to go to the fence as he nodded and said, "Yes, Nadya. Turtles."

"Cherepakha?" she said, more cautiously this time.

"I think that means 'turtle,' doesn't it?" he asked, and folded one hand over the other like a shell before poking out his thumb and wiggling it back and forth like a little head peeking out at the world. He held his hand-turtle out toward Nadya, and she giggled, sounding refreshingly like what he expected a little girl to sound like for the first time since they'd brought her home from the orphanage.

All the counselors they'd spoken to, both at the adoption agency and at the church, had warned them that children from state-run orphanages were often solemn, slow to trust that adults would have their best interests at heart, slower still to adjust to new surroundings. Factoring in the language and cultural barriers, it wasn't unreasonable to think it might be years, if ever, before Nadya trusted them. Hearing her laugh was a gift he hadn't been expecting to receive. He smiled, thumb bobbing up and down in parody of a nodding turtle.

"Hello," he said, making his voice deep and slow. "I am a turtle."

"Cherepakha," she said, obviously delighted.

"Cherepakha," he echoed, only mangling the word slightly. He pointed to one of the turtles. "Cherepakha."

Nadya beamed and bounced, clapping her hand against her thigh. It made sense, he supposed; she wanted to make a joyous noise, and she couldn't clap her hands together when she only had one hand. It still dimmed his joy a bit to be reminded that his new daughter, lovely as she was, would always be limited; they could give her all the advantages in the world, but they couldn't give her back her hand.

"Turtle," he said, still pointing. Nadya stopped bouncing and looked at him quizzically. "*Turtle,*" he repeated.

"Turtle," she said hesitantly.

This time, he bounced and clapped his hands against his legs, rather than hitting them together and reminding her of what she lacked (the idea that she might not think of herself as lacking *anything* had yet to form, and wouldn't for years yet; the idea that a child who didn't conform to his exact ideas of shape and function could be completely happy, and not consider herself lacking in the least, was even further away). This might not be the best means of language acquisition.

It was, however, a start.

NADYA'S NEW MOTHER WAS waiting when they returned from their walk, standing in the entryway with the note Nadya's new father had left on the fridge clutched in one hand. Nadya smiled at her hopefully as she removed her coat and hung it on the peg which she had been told, mainly through pantomime, belonged to her. Then she spun and threw her arms around the man's waist, giving him a brief but heartfelt hug, before running down the hall to her room.

The two adults were quiet until she was out of earshot. Then the woman asked, "Really, Carl? Taking her for outings without me? What happened to making sure she could accept us both? What happened to presenting a united front as a family?"

"She doesn't understand anything that's happened to her," he replied, voice only a little defensive. "We took her away from the only home she'd ever known and pulled her halfway around the world without asking her if she even wanted to go. So yeah, I took her for a walk while you were at the grocery store. That doesn't mean she's never going to accept you as her mother. She just wanted to see the turtles."

"She wanted to see the turtles, or you wanted to be the big hero who showed them to her?"

Carl threw his hands up in the air. "Come *on,* Pansy, we agreed we were going to do this together, and I'm still doing it with you! Can't you try doing it with me? Please?"

His wife, the love of his life, the woman who had reacted to the idea of adoption with immediate and enthusiastic buy-in as soon as their pastor suggested it, who was more than happy to give a little girl a better life in America, land of the free and home of the brave, continued looking at him coldly for long enough that he began to fear her answer. Maybe this wasn't going to work after all.

Finally, though, she sighed and said, "Our language classes are tonight. Don't forget. We're taking Nadya for pizza afterward."

Language night meant basic Russian for them—only enough to let them make themselves understood; not enough to allow Nadya to cling to her native tongue and refuse to integrate with her new home—and English as a second language for her, to help her adjust better and faster to life with her family. They knew they weren't equipped to teach a little girl who already spoke one language perfectly well how to speak English, and they needed her to be fluent if she was going to impress their church.

The Winslows had adopted a little boy from China, and he'd been speaking perfect English in less than a year. Nadya was smarter—she must have been, to survive that dreadful orphanage—and could be speaking English within six months, Pansy was absolutely sure of *that.* The idea of asking Nadya what *she* wanted had never occurred to either one of them. Children were people, absolutely, but foreign orphans were sure to be so consumed with gratitude that all they could possibly want was to make their new parents as happy as possible.

Peace made, Carl embraced his wife and walked with her into the kitchen. There was time to make all three of them sandwiches before it was time for language class.

3 LONG TIME PASSING

TIME PASSED, MORE HOURS slipping down the river, and Nadya adjusted, bit by bit, to her new reality. First the language classes, which were a punishment and a glory at the same time: the grammatical structure of English made no sense at all, and there was little poetry to the way words fit together. Still, being able to communicate her needs and desires to the people around her was worth any number of dull, leaden sentences sitting like ashes in her mouth; being able to understand and be understood was a gift so far beyond price that she didn't realize how much she had desired it until it was given to her.

The first day Nadya sat in her class and listened to her teacher speaking in slow, careful English and didn't need to request any direct translations, she cried. She sat at her desk and wept, and her instructor, a very nice woman who had become an ESL teacher out of a genuine desire to help people communicate, smiled in understanding and let her cry until the tears dried on their own.

Once the language classes were more about polish and refinement than actual base construction, it was time for speech classes, hour upon hour with a private tutor whose entire focus was the elimination of Nadya's accent. It was important, apparently, that she not be *too* foreign when she was meeting new people: they needed to look at her and understand that she had been plucked from another country, washed and pressed and molded into the perfect model of American childhood. Her teachers didn't have strong opinions about what *kind* of child she was going to be, as long as she was normal.

Six months after her arrival in Denver, Nadya was deemed ready to stand before a jury of her peers and be judged on her performance of American normalcy, and Carl and Pansy enrolled her in the local elementary school. The matrons at the orphanage had always put as much of a focus on education as they could, but they were understaffed and overstretched, and it hadn't been sufficient to keep the children where they needed to be. Nadya was reasonably up to where she was meant to be with math, but reading was essentially a matter of starting over from scratch, while history and geography both required forgetting most of what she already knew.

Relearning the history of the world from an Americentric perspective was technically no more difficult than any other part, but it was the most frustrating by far. Seeing achievements she had been taught mattered hugely reduced to a line in a textbook, if that, made her head ache, even as she buckled down and soldiered through as best as she could.

Life in the orphanage had taught her the value of obedience and grace, of listening to the people who swore they had her best interests at heart. By the time she finished with her language classes, she knew full well that Russia was farther away than she could ever hope to walk; this was her home now, if only because she had no place else that she could possibly go. And if she was going to live here, she needed to understand what that meant. She needed to belong. So she studied like she thought there was nothing in the world more important than the acquisition of knowledge, and when she got home at the end of her school days she would make her polite greetings to Carl and Pansy. They preferred to be called "Mom" and "Dad," and she was willing enough to go along with that, since respecting adults was always important. Once they were done asking her about her day, she would go to her room and do her homework as carefully and quickly as she could, because if she finished in time, she could go down to the pond and watch the turtles.

She was happy when she watched the turtles. They didn't look anything like her beloved Maksim—they were turtles, for one thing, and Carl had taken her to the pond on a translation error; Maksim was a tortoise. Although she supposed there wasn't a good place to go and watch tortoises all day, outside of a zoo. Turtles would suffice.

So they didn't look anything like home, but they were still turtles, slow until they needed to be fast, flat and long-necked and serene, completely adapted to their watery home. It was a simple thing, to be a turtle, and they were happy.

As long as she had the turtles, this could be home.

A year after she first came to America, Nadya had her first reason to question whether that was true. Pansy had picked her up from school, as was normal, and driven her to the doctor's office, which was slightly less normal, but was understandable, at least. It was within the realm of things that had been known to happen.

Carl was already there, waiting. That was strange. Nadya frowned, hanging back. Carl worked during the day, and was rarely home before dinner. For him to be there, at her doctor, hours before he should have been released . . . it was unusual at the very least. She had been in America by this point for long enough to understand more things than she had the year before. She knew how important work was to a man like Carl, and what an act of love and faith it had been to travel halfway around the world for the sake of bringing home a Russian orphan to be a part of his family. She knew doctors sometimes discussed things with parents that they wouldn't say to children, things that were thought to be too big for children to understand or accept. Maybe something was *wrong*. Maybe something inside her was sick or . . . or broken, and they were going to send her back to Russia, and . . .

And when did that become a bad thing? Nadya froze inside, allowing herself to be led into the office and seated on an exam table while she tried to think her way through the contradiction between desperately wanting to go home and loving her life here, with her private bedroom and her pond of turtles and her friends at school, who could be loud and wild and played with her at recess whenever she was brave enough.

Very few of them would have survived the orphanage, which made their childish, halting attempts at bullying easy to endure and dance around. They didn't know how to join forces against the bigger bullies, or how to coordinate a story to convince the teachers that they'd been doing something entirely and utterly innocent. They weren't her brothers and sisters like the children at the orphanage, but she would mold them soon enough, teaching them how to form a united front, teaching them their natural rage was better aimed outward, at teachers and authority figures, than inward at the weakest among them.

She was, in her own sideways, unintentional way, cultivating kindness, and she was doing it one day at a time, never quite seeming to understand what she was doing, focused only on her small student army and their need to control something, *anything*, about their surroundings.

She loved Russia. Russia was her mother, the first one

she ever knew. But when strangers had come from across an ocean, Russia had failed to protect her. Russia had looked at her and seen nothing of value, and allowed her to be taken by her new parents, her new family, to a new world and a new life, and much as she missed the orphanage, she knew many of the children she remembered would be gone by now, off to new families of their own, and the matrons would not be happy to see her returned. This life was all they had ever wanted for her.

She sat on the table and stared blankly straight ahead as the adults spoke, voices low and quick, making their still-unfamiliar words blend together into an undifferentiated stew of sounds. It's wasn't until the doctor lifted her right arm, turning it gently from side to side as he inspected her stump, that she came back into the present and tried to pull away.

The doctor's grip was tight enough that she couldn't break free without hurting herself. She turned a silent, pleading look on Carl and Pansy, hoping they would help her.

"Be a good girl, Nadya," said Pansy. "This is going to make you feel better."

Nadya stopped fighting the doctor and turned her eyes on him, gaze gone hard and unforgiving. He continued to turn her arm between his fingers, studying the structure of the stump.

When he let go, it was only to step back, adjust his glasses, and say, "Yes, this should be an easy procedure."

Nadya blinked at him. "What will be?"

"It's a fairly standard model, no truly fine motor dexterity, but the technology is advancing every day. We'll be able to do bone implants in a few years, give her something that provides the illusion of feeling. Since she's not in any active distress, this will be primarily cosmetic. It should be ready in a week."

"Wonderful, thank you so much," said Pansy, beaming. She turned to Nadya. "Thank the nice doctor, Nadya."

"Thank you, doctor," said Nadya obediently. She didn't know what she was thanking him for, but adults who were demanding politeness rarely wanted to discuss their reasons why. Besides, this was apparently all they'd come to the doctor's office to do; Carl was offering her coat, a twinkle in his eye.

"We'll stop for ice cream on the way home," he said, conspiratorially.

Nadya giggled. She liked ice cream. She liked ice cream a *lot*. They had ice cream in Russia, of course, but not often; there were always better things to spend the orphanage budget on than sweet treats for the children. She let her coat be slipped over her shoulders, let Carl take her hand and lead her to the door while Pansy finished talking to the doctor, both of them once again speaking too fast and too low for Nadya to understand.

Then Pansy joined them, and together the three of them left the office, heading for the elevators. Pansy managed to keep her quiet until they were almost to the ground floor. Then she looked at Nadya, frowning, and said, "Well, say something."

"Um, hello?" said Nadya.

"She means about your arm," said Carl.

Nadya blinked. "What about my arm?"

The elevator stopped. Pansy stepped out and did the same, standing in the middle of the elevator lobby as she turned on her daughter and asked, "Did you understand anything that just happened? Were you paying any attention at all?"

"Yes, I was paying attention, no, I did not understand why we had to come and see a new doctor," said Nadya. "I like the woman who gives me the shots. She always lets me have a sweet when she's done. A suck-pop. I enjoy the suck-pops."

"I don't even know where to begin with that," said Pansy, and turned to Carl. "You handle her. I'll be in the car."

Then she stomped away, and Carl was alone with his daughter, who looked up at him with despairing confusion in her eyes. He knelt down, to be more on a level.

"All right, pumpkin, you know how most little girls your age have two arms?"

"Yes," said Nadya, surprised. Of course she knew that. She paid attention to people, she owned several dolls, and she would have noticed long since if one and a half had somehow become the standard number of arms. "I don't because the doctor says my mother was probably exposed to something teratogenic while she was pregnant with me, and it's a miracle that everything else about me is as perfect as it is."

"Can't remember 'lollipop,' but can say 'teratogenic,'" murmured Carl, who did that fairly frequently, making comments like she couldn't understand him if he kept his voice low. Nadya didn't mind, though. It was better than Pansy, who rolled her eyes and stomped away, not explaining herself at all.

It was as if she thought that teaching a child English and eliminating as much of her accent as possible was like pressing the reset button on their upbringing and culture, and could transform Nadya into an American child overnight.

"Yes," said Nadya, uncertainly.

Carl seemed to remember that she was there. He smiled encouragingly and said, "Well, we know the other children can be cruel."

How could they know that? They had never been to her school during classes, never seen the way the children interact. Unless the assumption was that all American children will be cruel, that they somehow can't help themselves, which seemed unfair. Some of the children she went to school with had to be taught not to abuse those smaller than themselves, but they were all quick studies, and she had seen little cruelty from the children themselves. She blinked at him in slow bewilderment, waiting for him to start making sense.

"We wanted to make sure you'd be comfortable, and we wanted it to be as much of a surprise as possible, so you wouldn't have to wait too long." He paused, apparently waiting for her to catch on and get excited, then sighed a little and said, "We've bought you a new arm."

Nadya blinked again, slow and deliberate. "But I have an arm," she said, and raised her left hand toward him, palm outward and fingers spread, so he could see the whole thing.

"This is what's called a prosthetic arm," he said. "It goes over your right arm, so it will be the same length as your left. You'll have a hand, too, although you won't be able to use it."

"Protez?" asked Nadya, and was suddenly glad that Pansy had already stalked away. Her accent might have been wiped into obscurity when she spoke English, but when she spoke Russian, even short words, it came rushing right back like the tide. She swallowed, forcing her tongue back to American patterns, and said, "I am fine. I do not need a protez—a, ah, prosthetic—arm. I am happy as I am."

"But you can't be," Carl insisted. "You must want to be a whole little girl."

Nadya paused. Why did she have to want that? She did perfectly well with one hand and one stump that she could use for gripping things when necessary; the world rarely demanded more of her than that. The things she couldn't do for herself were few and far between, and most of them were things she could live without. She didn't need to polish her own nails when it was easy enough to convince the other girls to do it for her, and the hand she had was more than steady enough to let her reciprocate. She could play tetherball and kickball, and she got to sit out dodgeball, which didn't look like it would be all that much fun *anyway*. So there was nothing she could think of, really, that would be easier or better with two hands, especially when one of them wouldn't even work.

"I do not," she said, politely. "Thank you, though. I'm happy precisely as I am."

Carl looked at her sadly.

ONE WEEK LATER, they were back in the doctor's office, Pansy and Carl watching as the doctor strapped Nadya's new prosthetic onto her right arm. He talked very slowly and carefully as he did, explaining how she could put it on and take it off by herself, how it would probably be easier, at first, if she slid it through her sleeves before putting her shirts on in the morning, and that she shouldn't get it wet, but that she'd get used to it soon enough.

"After a little while, you'll wonder how you could ever have gotten along without it," he said jovially, and Nadya offered him a polite smile and didn't contradict him. Contradicting adults so often ended badly. She hadn't gotten her ice cream after their last visit to his office, and if the prosthetic arm was an inescapable future, she at least wanted it to be an inescapable future with ice cream.

She couldn't feel the arm, of course, and she couldn't move

the hand, but there was a simple lever of sorts inside the attachment point, which she could control by flexing her stump. So she raised her arm and flexed her stump, and watched with wide eyes as the unfamiliar arm swung forward, bending at the elbow to form a perfect angle. She unflexed and the arm straightened again.

"As you get older, we'll be able to fit you with more advanced models," said the doctor. "You'll also develop the muscles that allow you to manipulate the arm by doing it, and that will make those advanced models easier for you to use. Everything feeds into everything else, after all."

Nadya lowered her new arm and nodded at him gravely.

Then, again, it was time for Carl and Pansy to talk about her like she wasn't there, voices bright and rapid, the doctor answering technical questions she couldn't even begin to understand. Normally, when the three of them walked together, they walked with her in the middle, where passersby couldn't see and possibly comment on her missing arm. Today, as they walked to the elevators, Pansy made sure she was at the outside, her new right arm facing toward the world.

Nadya had never felt so much like a trinket or a prize. She ducked her head and did her best to keep up, almost walking into the elevator door.

"Honestly, Nadya, watch where you're going!" said Pansy. "If you give yourself a bloody nose, we won't be able to go for ice cream before dinner."

"Yes, Mom," said Nadya softly.

"And keep your head up. People will think we beat you."

"Yes, Mom," said Nadya, and adjusted her posture, head up, shoulders down, trying to look like she liked this, like she was completely confident and comfortable and content. The new prosthetic itched and chafed where it rubbed against her skin; even all the talcum and lotion in the world couldn't change the fact that she had never intentionally strapped anything to her arm before, never seen herself as lesser because she only had one hand, never seen the need to transform into something more. This was not her choice. This was her body, but it was not her decision, and that alone made it very heavy, and difficult to carry.

They went out to the car as a family, Nadya buckling herself into the back seat after bending her new arm carefully up, out of the way. She supposed she could see why many people would think of this as a good thing, especially people who had misplaced the arms they started out with: it was somewhat nice to have an even weight on both sides of her body, keeping her right shoulder from drifting upward as she walked (a habit which had caused more than one matron to comment on how she would develop a hunch if she wasn't careful). And having a second hand to lay across the strap did make it easier to click the buckle home.

Still, it wasn't something she'd ever wanted, and it itched and pulled and ached as she sat in the back and fought the urge to fidget. Carl didn't care when she fidgeted, said she was the one in back and he was the one in front, so whatever she wanted to do with her own space was fine by him, but Pansy took it remarkably personally when Nadya seemed to be anything less than perfectly content.

Privately, Nadya thought *Pansy* was less than perfectly content, and maybe shouldn't have been allowed to have authority over another human being until she figured out how to be kinder to herself. But that was a large, complicated thought that would have needed some large, complicated words to articulate, and all the large, complicated words she had were in Russian, making them difficult to use with her new parents. Both of them had dutifully attended their Russian language classes for the first six months Nadya was with them, and could now carry on a simple conversation in her mother tongue. That didn't mean they were willing to actually *do* it. Neither of them had spoken a word of Russian outside of family court since the day she was judged fluent enough to communicate in English.

They were doing their best to erase her roots. Nadya considered that with more gravity than most would expect from a ten-year-old girl as they drove to the ice cream parlor, as she selected her cone—cookies and cream, with sprinkles—and as they sat at the tables outside, a perfect little family in a perfect little display. They wanted her to be their all-American girl, and to replace her missing parts with pieces of their own design.

It would be easy enough to let them do it, to sit back and allow Nadezhda Sokolov to be replaced by Nadya Sanders. It wouldn't hurt. If she didn't resist, she probably wouldn't even notice it happening, and it would make Carl so happy. It would please Pansy, too, but she cared less about pleasing Pansy: Pansy knew the little girl she had wanted better than the little girl she had, and never took Nadya to see the turtles either at home or on their family outings to the zoo. When Carl had raised the idea that Nadya might benefit from a pet in the home, and suggested a tortoise, Pansy had been the one to say that she would never have a filthy reptile in her house, and that a cat would be much better for a growing girl.

Nadya didn't understand quite how an animal that pooped in a box of sand would be less dirty than a tortoise, which was quiet and didn't jump or scratch the furniture, even though it would occasionally defecate in its own water dish, but she had already learned that it was better not to argue. They were going to get a cat at Christmas, according to Pansy's careful schedule, something soft and fluffy and beautiful.

Nadya was less excited about this than she knew she was expected to be. So no, pleasing Pansy wasn't her first priority. But pleasing Carl could be a good thing, and could make her life, which was already easier and more luxurious than she had ever dreamt it could be, easier still. All she had to do was give in.

Nadezhda Sokolov had not survived nine years as a one-armed girl in a state-run orphanage by being timid or easy to push around. She ate her ice cream and privately pledged resistance. She rode home with her new parents, still pledging resistance, and went to her room with her new prosthetic arm hanging heavy by her side.

When she removed it for bed, the skin where it had been rubbing was red and angry. She touched it gently with her fingertips before getting the lotion the doctor had recommended, and knew that resistance was only the beginning.

PART II

INTO THE DEEP DEPTHS

4 ONE-ARMED GIRLS NEED SWIMMING LESSONS TOO

NADYA WAS REQUIRED to wear her arm to school, the way a child who had recently been fitted with their first pair of glasses might be required to wear their glasses. She had tried objecting, only to be informed that a properly grateful little girl would understand and appreciate what was being done for her, not make her parents' lives more difficult by complaining when she had nothing to complain about.

As always, Pansy had played the bad cop while Carl looked placidly on, not supporting his wife but not objecting, either. Nadya had pled and tried her very best to explain her objections, all for naught, because she was small and they were large and they were *helping*. How could she be so ungrateful as to refuse to let them *help*?

So she was whisked away to school with the unfamiliar weight of the new arm hanging heavy from her shoulder and pinching her skin, and that day the other students looked at her like she was somehow broken for the very first time. They had grown accustomed to overlooking Nadya's missing arm, seeing absence as a part of her body; having an arm suddenly appear was worth staring at. What's more, the arm was visibly artificial, and Nadya was visibly uncomfortable.

She wasn't the only child in school with a prosthetic; one of the boys in fifth grade had a prosthetic leg, and they were all used to Michael. He didn't even walk with a limp most of the time, save for right before he was fitted for an improvement. And one of the teachers had a prosthetic eye, which one student or another would periodically claim they had seen her remove and drop into a glass of water. So while a few of the other students might have been staring with intent to mock, the majority were simply fascinated by the appearance of something new in their environment.

Nadya loved going to the zoo with Carl and Pansy, even if Pansy found most of the animals loud and unattractive, and just wanted to look at birds and tigers all the time. And one of the concepts she liked best was the idea that every animal, from the biggest or the smallest, had zookeepers assigned to something called an "enrichment team." Those were the people whose job it was to find them new toys, new things to taste and smell, new ways to keep their enclosures interesting and engaging, so they wouldn't get bored and start breaking things for fun.

She thought, sometimes, that she and all the other students were part of a massive mutual enrichment team. They gave each other something new to look at every single day, keeping them from succumbing to boredom and destroying their enclosure.

And today, thanks to her new arm, she was the something new. She'd been the something new once before, when she first arrived at the school. She hadn't liked it then, and she didn't like it now.

She squirmed through her morning classes, fidgeted through recess, and, when lunch arrived, rushed to the cafeteria to be at the front of the lunch line, grabbing her tray as she always did, only to discover that her new arm interfered with the way she would normally brace it against her body. She staggered, unable to use the arm to support the tray even without the weight of her lunch, unable to get the tray between her arm and her body. It was only when one of the other students stepped in and helped her that she was able to get to her lunch and head for the table where she usually sat. Her cheeks burned the whole way. It was rare for her to need help with basic tasks, and while she had been warned that there would be a period of adjustment, she wasn't used to feeling helpless.

Nadya sat at the table, picking at her macaroni and cheese, and hated her new arm a little bit more than she had before the bell rang. One of the boys prodded her in the shoulder and asked a question about her prosthetic. She answered softly, barely aware of her own words, and bent her arm at his request, demonstrating the way the elbow bent when she flexed her stump. The other kids began talking enthusiastically about the arm, how cool it was, how lucky she was to have it, and didn't seem to notice that they weren't talking about *her* anymore at all. They weren't talking *to* her, either; like a room full of kindergarteners with a fun new toy, they were talking about the toy.

It was *her* assistance device, *her* mechanism for better interacting with the world, not a replacement for who she was as a person. She'd never really considered her missing arm a disability—it was just the way she was made, and always had been, and it didn't stop her from doing anything she wanted to do—and now it was all the other children could see.

She didn't like it. It burned.

They finished lunch and rose, an amorphous group of second-graders on their way to the playground. Nadya moved within the pack, as she so often did, neither hanging back nor pushing her way to the front. Her stump ached. She wanted to remove the arm and rub more lotion into her skin, but she didn't dare attract attention to the arm again: it would only cause the other kids to focus on it, when she desperately didn't want them to.

"Dodgeball," said one of the boys. "Since Nadya can finally play!"

Nadya blinked and protested. She couldn't "play," as they said, couldn't hold or catch or throw the ball any better than she'd been able to the day before. But she could be pulled to the dodgeball court, and she could use her hands—both the one she was born with and the one she was wearing—to bat the balls out of the way as they came rocketing toward her. The other kids laughed and laughed, and if most of them liked her and didn't understand how they were making her unhappy in fundamental, unkind ways, they were still young enough not to understand all the possible forms of cruelty. Nadya dodged and twisted as well as she could, but was still hit by several red rubber balls before the bell rang again to end lunch and they all went trooping back to the classroom, where she hunched in her seat and stared at her paper, and hated.

Oh, how she hated. She hated being forced to conform to other people's idea of normal, whether they be cultural or physical. She hated how easy it was for the adults in her world to pass her around like a doll, moving her from Russia to America, from house to doctor's office, from her bedroom to wherever they wanted her to be. She hated that her agency had been taken away from her in ways she couldn't fully articulate, and she sat at her desk, and she seethed.

Until the bell ran for the end of the day, and she rose, gathered her things, and scooted for the door as fast as her legs would take her, not pausing until she was at the bus-stop line. Once there, she waited anxiously, jiggling her weight from foot to foot, counting the seconds until the big yellow bus pulled up and she could climb aboard, ready to head for home. They had to wait while the children who were in less of a hurry came out of the school and got onto the bus. Nadya squirmed deeper and deeper into her seat, self-conscious in a way she couldn't remember ever having been before, right arm pressed up against the bus wall where no one would poke at it, or stare, or ask questions she didn't want to answer yet. How was she supposed to tell people how she felt when she didn't know yet how she felt?

The bus pulled away from the stop with a lurch. Nadya closed her eyes. They were on the way home. She was safe.

When they reached her stop, she got off the bus without saying anything, staring down the block at the square, comfortable shape of the house she shared with her adoptive parents. If she squinted, eyelashes laced together like the fingers on folded hands, she could blur the outline enough to make it resemble the orphanage, which might not be well-beloved but was certainly familiar. She knew who she was at the orphanage. She knew who she was expected to be. She looked down at the artificial palm of her right hand, eyes still half-closed, and through the blur, it looked almost real.

But she wasn't a girl with a right hand. She was a girl without one. It had never defined her, but it had always been a true part of who she was, as true as her dark brown hair and lighter eyes, as true as her slightly snaggled left incisor. All the little pieces of a person. She didn't know how to be this new version of herself.

It was a transition many had weathered before her, and many would weather after, and had her new parents ever considered that perhaps a girl who'd never *had* a hand might not *miss* having a hand and taken steps to help her through the process, she might have taken it as smoothly as some of them. But Carl and Pansy had been looking for a child, partially because their pastor said it was their proper Christian duty and partially because they thought they ought to want one, and now here she was, lost, with two adults who barely understood what it was to be responsible for another living being.

Nadya blinked away the beginning of tears and trudged toward the house, right arm dangling by her side and left hand clutching the strap of her backpack, keeping it from slipping down her shoulder. Pansy's car was in the driveway as Nadya let herself in, stepping out of her shoes before heading down the hall toward her room.

"How was your first day?" asked Pansy, appearing in the kitchen doorway.

Nadya stopped and looked at her in confusion. She had been at this school since September, and they wouldn't change classes until *next* September. "It was . . . fine," she said, having learned that positive but noncommittal answers would usually free her from the burden of parental expectation, confusing or not, more quickly. Pansy was still looking at her expectantly. "We're doing multiplication in math. After I finish my homework, may I go to the turtle pond?"

"I don't want to hear about your homework, I want to hear about how the other kids reacted to your *arm*," said Pansy, now sounding annoyed.

Ah. So this was another scripted conversation, then, and as usual, Nadya was on the wrong foot because she hadn't learned her lines. She never did. She still forced a smile, and said, "They found it very interesting. Michael, who's three years ahead of me, has a prosthetic leg, and he plays kickball all the time. I played dodgeball for the first time today." The bruises were already forming.

Still, she kept smiling and waiting to hear that she had finally managed to say enough, to satisfy Pansy's insatiable desire to be the one who did things correctly, the one everyone looked at and said "There, that woman, she's a good woman, a pious woman, devoted to her family, she's the one I want to be like." And to her great relief, Pansy relaxed and nodded, saying, "Your homework comes first, but after that, yes you can go to the turtle pond, as long as you finish at least an hour before dinner. Come and give me a hug."

"Yes, Mom," said Nadya, and trotted obediently over to hug Pansy with her left arm, resolutely ignoring the disappointment on the other woman's face at her failure to use both. Pulling away, she walked down the hall to her room, leaving Pansy watching after her.

Pansy sighed and shook her head as Nadya vanished into her room. She was trying so hard to understand the girl, but nothing they ever did seemed to be good enough for her. She was serious all the time, seeming to look toward a future that she had yet to share with either of the adults who cared for her. She'd expected an orphan overflowing with gratitude over being offered a better life, and had thought Nadya would absolutely embody that spirit when she'd first seen her among the other children, a bright-eyed little director gleefully organizing them according to her own design. How had that child become the one they had? It didn't make any sense.

In her room, Nadya pulled books out of the backpack and dropped them onto the small desk provided for her use. She couldn't think of any of the furnishings as "hers": they had all been selected *for* her, not *by* her, and while she liked them well enough, they were much more suited to Pansy's tastes than her own. That was all right: she'd never been able to pick her own things at the orphanage, either. But it just fed into the feeling that she was there to be a prop, not to be a person, and one day she'd be replaced by a little girl who did a better, faster job of conforming to Pansy and Carl's unspoken, sometimes nebulous expectations.

That little girl would probably think this room was perfect exactly as it was. She wouldn't dream of changing a thing. And if they bought *her* a prosthetic arm, she would be grateful to have it, not dubiously unsure that she wanted anything of the sort, not squirming when it rubbed against her skin. She would be a grateful, dutiful daughter, and they would forget Nadya entirely.

Nadya wished her well, even as she hurried through her homework and put it carefully back in her backpack, ready to be turned in the next day. She lived here now; even if this wasn't going to be her home forever, it was still hers, and she would live with all its sharp edges and strangeness. She would be strong. That was what the matrons would have wanted her to be, what the other children would have expected from her, what Russia would have demanded of her, if Russia had been in a position to demand anything.

Russia had, after all, repeated the one crime for which Nadya had never been able to fully forgive her first mother. Russia had given her away when she was too much to care for.

Leaving her room, Nadya padded back down the hall to her shoes, relieved when Pansy didn't appear again. Sometimes, permission to go out would be rescinded in favor of chores, especially when Nadya was going to see the turtles, which was unladylike and, in Pansy's eyes, unnecessary. But her day had been long and unpleasant in strange new ways—ways she couldn't help remembering as the unfamiliar weight of her new arm bumped against her side—and she needed the turtles.

Stepping back into her shoes, Nadya took her coat from the hook and stepped out into the crisp afternoon air, beginning what had long since become a familiar walk through their small housing development to the turtle pond. It had been a warm enough day that several of the turtles were basking when she arrived, and she paused, squinting at their round, familiar bodies, a flame of rage kindling in her soul.

Someone had taken a knife or a rock—something sharp, anyway—and scratched two words into the shell of the largest turtle currently basking on the log. But a shell wasn't just a piece of clothing or a pack the turtle carried! It was the turtle's *body,* naked to the world!

It took a moment for her rage to clear enough for the words to actually register: *byt' uveren.* A beat later, she realized why that looked so strange, apart from words having no business on the back of a turtle.

They were written in Russian. *Be sure.* Be sure of what? Be sure it was a crime to scratch words into a turtle? Because she was absolutely sure of *that.* Still candle-bright with rage, Nadya ducked under the top bar of the fence and stepped onto the narrow strip of bare earth between it and the pond itself. The turtles were used to her by now, and watched her with slow, wise eyes, not abandoning their perch. What could one child do to them from a distance? She wasn't one of the children who liked to throw rocks or poke with sticks. She was safe.

Nadya began inching her way around the pond, trying to watch her footing and the turtles at the same time. Had someone asked in that moment what she was intending to do, she wouldn't have been able to give them a good answer. But she couldn't just walk away, not when the turtle was so clearly injured. She had to *help.*

On the log, the turtles looked at each other, nodding in slow symphony, like they had reached a reptilian consensus. One by one, they dropped into the water.

The turtle with the words etched into its shell was the last to move, shifting position so that it was closer to Nadya as she moved along the bank. It watched her progress, watched as her eyes fell on the cattails and rushes that grew dense in the clear water, reaching for the sky, watched as those same eyes went terribly wide. Nadya stared.

She was used to seeing patterns in things where adults would insist there were no patterns, rabbits in the clouds and dancing bears in the shapes of leaves. But she had never seen a half-open door etched in waterweeds before. It looked oddly inviting, like it wanted her to step through it. But she couldn't do that, because it wasn't a door; it was just . . . a shape in the water, just an outline of something that wasn't real.

She was so busy staring at the door that wasn't that she didn't notice how close she was to the edge, or how the ground under her foot had started to crumble, until she lost her balance and fell forward with a yelp, crashing into the water at the direct center point of the door that wasn't there. The splash was surprisingly soft.

She didn't resurface.

After a few seconds had passed, the turtle with the scratched-up shell dropped into the water, following her lead, and swam away.

5 ON THE BANKS OF THE WINSOME RIVER

NADYA WOKE WET AND ACHING, clothes plastered to her body by drying pondwater and sticky silt. She pulled her face away from the muddy bank where she was resting, coughing and spitting out a bit of grit, and rolled onto her back, staring up at the sky.

It was gray and heavy with pendulous clouds, their bellies swollen with rain yet to fall. She blinked, frowning at that sky. It didn't look right. She hadn't seen clouds like that since arriving in Denver. Even on the rare occasions when it rained, the clouds weren't the deep, lowland clouds of her early childhood, the clouds she remembered from the orphanage. These clouds looked pregnant with storm, ripe and ready to begin throwing lightning from one to the next, to roll with thunder as they sheeted rain down on the land beneath them.

These weren't Russian clouds, either, not quite, but they were closer than she'd seen in a long time, and they filled her heart with lightness, even as her hair was filled with muck. Her hair . . .

Pansy was going to kill her.

She sat up abruptly, the fingers of her hand digging into the mud, eyes so wide it hurt, looking frantically around in a vague attempt to figure out how long she'd been floating in the pond. Her panic didn't recede as she realized she didn't recognize anything around her. Instead, it built and pooled behind her breastbone, becoming something dark and terrible that threatened to break loose and sweep her away. It was a raging flood, and the dam holding it at bay was very thin indeed, barely worthy of the name.

Nadya pushed herself to her feet and considered the scene in front of her. She had washed up on the bank of a wide, rolling river that stretched out in both directions as far as she could see. The edges were a verdant wonderland of reeds and grasses, with small trees forming copses here and there, dotted along the length of the water like a deconstructed forest. On the other side of the river was a narrow stretch of muddy ground, followed by a second river, narrower than the first but rushing just as swiftly . . . in the opposite direction.

Nadya blinked. She had always assumed rivers ran the way they did because of gravity or the location of the sea or the angle of the land or something else mundane and immutable like that. She had never seen two rivers in close proximity flowing in opposite directions at the same time before. It seemed oddly impossible.

She turned and looked behind her, and saw that the land there was completely covered in trees, an *actual* forest to complement the one that had almost managed to take root along the river's edge. It looked marshy and soft, though, and she could tell without trying that if she were to walk into it, the ground would be muddy enough to suck the shoes off her feet before she took more than a few steps. When the clouds split and doused the world, the river would swell and the forest would flood. It was at least halfway to being a swamp. While she had never heard the term "flooded forest" before, she would have known it immediately for the correct way to describe what she was looking at.

Nadya turned again, back to the original river. She couldn't understand how she'd arrived there. The last thing she remembered was falling through the door in the pond, the water filling her nose and mouth and dimming the world as she frantically thrashed with both arms. But swimming lessons had never been a priority at the orphanage, and Pansy and Carl had yet to even offer them to her. Most people assumed she would never be able to learn to swim, and being able to join the turtles in the water had been one of the few hopes born from the acquisition of her new arm.

But it had been too new, and she hadn't known how to use it, and she had fallen too fast. She must have breathed the water in and lost consciousness. She hadn't drowned, she was fairly sure of that: drowned girls didn't stand and look at rivers, or think about how much trouble they were going to be in when they got home. They certainly didn't have silt in their underpants or caught under the lip of their uncomfortable prosthetic arms. Nadya fumbled to find and unfasten the straps, giving a small sigh of relief when the arm fell away from her stump and let her chafed, aching skin breathe.

The skin had started to redden and blister around the line where the false arm attached to her real one. She rubbed it idly with her hand, trying to ease some of the ache away. It helped, although not as much as she wanted it to. She frowned at the river.

The river burbled on.

"Hello?" called Nadya experimentally, bending to retrieve the prosthetic arm from the mud where it had fallen. "Is there anyone there?"

No one answered, the river least of all. She sighed. Apparently, she was well and truly alone in the middle of nowhere, far enough from home that she wouldn't be able to walk back there before anyone noticed she was gone. Even if she could, they would surely notice that she was soaked to the skin and muddy, and that would be enough to get her into trouble. It wasn't fair, really. She would never have gone past the fence if someone hadn't hurt that poor turtle, and if she hadn't gone past the fence, she wouldn't have been able to fall into the pond, even if she lost her balance! This wasn't her fault at all, it was the fault of whoever thought it would be funny to write on a turtle!

As she fumed over the indignity of it all, something fell from the clouds above her and dropped toward the river like a stone, plummeting into the water. Nadya blinked, first at the falling object and then up at the clouds.

They had parted just a little where the object had come through, allowing her a glimpse of what should have been the sky on the other side. But instead of sky, it looked like a shimmering sheet of water, liquid and rippling like the surface of the pond in the afternoon sun. Then the clouds surged shut again, and the glimpse of water-sky was gone. Nadya kept staring at the place where it had been, trying to wrap her head around the impossibility of it all.

Something splashed in the water in front of her. She snapped around and saw a frog the size of a small horse come hopping out of the river, bulbous eyes blinking. Nadya blinked back. She didn't know, exactly, how large it was possible for frogs to be, but she was quite sure she had never seen a frog this big, not even at the zoo. Not even in books.

The frog's eyes flattened down into its head every time it blinked, a comic sight that made Nadya start to giggle. She tried to put her hand over her mouth, only to almost smack herself in the face with the prosthetic arm she was holding. That just made her giggle harder. This was all ridiculous and impossible, and now there was a giant *frog*. How could she do anything *but* laugh? It was too silly to do anything else!

The frog stopped blinking and hopped closer to her. Nadya watched it come, still giggling. The frog looked so funny when it moved. Did all frogs look this funny when they moved? Maybe she had just never noticed before.

The frog seemed to tense somehow, like it was drawing in on itself. Nadya frowned, feeling strangely threatened by the change in the frog's posture. It didn't look any less ridiculous than it had a moment before, but it looked *dangerous* all tensed up like that, like a cartoon character that was about to produce a mallet out of nowhere.

"Hello, Mr. Frog?" said Nadya anxiously. She tried again in Russian. She didn't know why a frog might be more likely to speak Russian than English, but she didn't know how a frog could look dangerous, either, and this one did. Better to cover all her bases.

The frog opened its mouth and its tongue came out. Not like in the cartoons, where frogs had impossibly long tongues that could snatch insects out of the air from improbably far away, but like it was flopping out of the frog's mouth, like it was structurally somehow *wrong*, as if it had been anchored in the wrong part of the mouth. Nadya only had a moment to register the wrongness of the frog's tongue—which was a small thing, given the wrongness of literally everything else—before that tongue made contact with her prosthetic arm and yanked it back, out of her hands, into the frog's mouth, which snapped viciously shut.

Nadya froze completely, torn between the urge to run and scream and the urge to charge the frog and demand the return of her property. She would probably have run before the second thought could fully form, but she had already been told, firmly, that the prosthetic was expensive. She wasn't to remove it when she wasn't in her own room, safely away from any opportunities to lose it. Feeding it to a giant frog more than certainly qualified as losing it.

The frog's throat bulged as it swallowed, eyes closing again. In that moment, Nadya saw her opportunity for escape. It would mean leaving the arm behind, but the mouth that swallowed her arm was certainly more than large enough to follow it up with a little girl. But the frog couldn't stick its tongue out while it had something in its mouth, and it had to close its eyes to swallow. She remembered reading that in a book.

Keeping her eyes on the frog, she bent and picked up a rock from the riverbank, the largest one she was confident that she could lift. Then she took a step backward and held the rock at arm's length, wiggling it as invitingly as she could. What would a frog find inviting? Hopefully, a rock being shaken back and forth by an anxious little girl.

The frog's tongue shot out again, brushing her fingers with sticky dampness as it collided with the rock. Nadya let go immediately, and when the frog swallowed, eyes closing, she spun and bolted for the forest. She couldn't get the arm back if she was *inside* the frog. Worrying about how much trouble she was going to get into when she got home was silly when there was a chance she was never going to get home at all.

The frog hopped after her, every impact of its body with the ground making a wet squelching noise that was going to haunt her dreams. Nadya kept running, and when she reached the muddy edge of the trees, she plunged between them, running as hard as she could for the narrowest spaces in sight.

She dove through several gaps, barely squeezing through the smallest of them, before she turned and looked back. The frog was a considerable distance behind her, unable to fit between the trees and follow her into the wood. She was safe, for now. But she couldn't go back, and going deeper into the forest would mean admitting she was well and truly lost, and intending to stay that way.

The frog watched her as she moved through the forest, shifting its weight from one massive leg to another, and she knew down to the bones of her that her choice was an illusion. Deeper was the only way left to go.

And so she went.

6 INTO THE FLOODED FOREST

THE SOIL IN THE FOREST was as soft and spongy as Nadya had assumed it would be, and once the fear of the frog faded, she slowed down and began choosing a more careful path through the trees, trying to hop between the patches of almost-dry ground. The tree roots helped; often, she could balance atop them, placing her feet gingerly in a straight line as she inched her way along.

The rain might come frequently, but it hadn't come for at least a day; the ground was only this wet because the trees blocked most of whatever sun could filter through the gray, gravid clouds. Without heat, the water didn't evaporate, just lingered and sank slowly through the saturated ground. Patches of moss grew lush and green, dotted with tiny white flowers, and spiny bushes put forth flowers of their own, branches heavy with round red berries. Mushrooms and toadstools clustered around the bottoms of the trees, their tops white and smooth or red and speckled or purple and glowing.

Nadya looked around with wide eyes as she walked, taking note of everything, touching nothing but the trunks of the trees. The wilderness could hold many dangers, she knew, and she didn't want to find herself in more trouble than she already was.

This was going to be a hard story to convince Carl and Pansy of when she got home. "I fell into the pond, and then I was somehow on a riverbank, and then a giant frog ate my arm and chased me into a big, wet forest" didn't sound like a real thing that could have happened to a real person, least of all to her.

Nadya kept walking until her legs began to ache. The forest seemed to go on forever, as wide as the river was long, and she hadn't been able to see the end of the river in either direction, no matter how hard she squinted. Nothing moved in the trees. The frog was far behind her now, and she was safely alone.

Wrapping her arms around herself, Nadya sank into a crouching position at the base of the nearest tree, shivering and shuddering, trying to ride the fear as it swept over her in a crushing wave. She was alone. She was lost in this strange place, and she was *alone.* No matter how far she walked, that wasn't going to change unless she found other people, and to do that, she would have to find her way out of the forest, and what if there was another frog waiting to gobble her down, quick as the first one had swallowed her arm? She was tired and she was cold and her clothes were wet and sticking to her, uncomfortably, and her feet hurt and the stump of her arm hurt and she was hungry and getting hungrier. Soon, she'd be hungry enough for the mushrooms to start looking like food, and she knew enough about the wilderness to know that people who ate wild mushrooms didn't have long lives ahead of them.

She was going to die here. There was no way around it. She shook and shuddered, trying to sob without making a sound. If there *was* anything in this wood to attract, she didn't want to meet it.

"Stop your weeping, human child," said a voice, close to her ear. It was a thin voice, lacking substance somehow, like the lungs behind it weren't very strong. Nadya jerked upright, taking her forearm away from her eyes, whipping around to see who had spoken.

The words were in English. Someone had found her, someone *must* have found her, she wasn't lost anymore, she—

She was looking at a small fox with tawny reddish-gold fur and a white blaze across its chest and the lower part of its muzzle, sitting on a nearby tree root with its bushy tail wrapped securely around its paws. It tracked the motion of her head with its sharp golden eyes, and it was hard not to feel as if it knew exactly what it was looking at.

"Hello?" called Nadya, looking away from the fox. "Is there someone there?"

"*I'm* here, and you were just looking at me, so you'd think you would know that," said the voice, sounding less than amused. Nadya's head snapped back around. She stared at the fox. The fox stared back.

Several long seconds passed like this, until the fox yawned enormously, showing a great many sharp white teeth, and hopped off the tree root to the marshy ground. "Fine," it said, as it went. "If you aren't interested in civil conversation, I'll be on my way, and you can go back to watering the mushrooms."

"No!" blurted Nadya, raising her hand in a beseeching gesture. The fox stopped and looked at her. "Please. Please don't go. I just . . . Where I come from, foxes don't talk." Not outside of stories, anyway. She'd heard plenty of stories about talking foxes, and stories had to come from somewhere, didn't they? Stories had to have beginnings, which meant someone had to *be* where they were beginning, or there was no purpose to them. She was just at the beginning of a story, that was all, and this was perfectly possible.

The fox continued looking at her for a long moment,

seeming, in a sharp, vulpine way, to take her measure. Then it trotted back to the tree and hopped back up onto the root where it had been sitting before. "Very well, as long as you hold my interest," it said. "Do you have a name, human child? And what has become of your arm?"

"My name is Nadezhda," said Nadya, because here, it still could be; she had the feeling that no one in this vast and flooded forest would care what she called herself, or if that name felt foreign on their tongues. "The frog that came out of the river took my arm and swallowed it."

"Dreadful things, frogs," said the fox. "Mostly stomach, with just enough leg attached to fling themselves at the food. And for a frog, 'food' means whatever they can fit into their mouths, which are large outside of all reason. No, you were right to run away from a frog large enough to take a human's arm. I would have run as well. We can't all be heroes, after all. World's not looking for one at the moment, so far as I'm aware."

"What would a hero have done?"

"A hero would have found a way to fight the frog, to be sure it couldn't take the arms off of anyone else. Can't have a community without any arms at all. I mean, I have no arms, as you humans measure them, but I need my legs. I can get about just fine with one injured paw. Hurt two of them, and whew." The fox whistled, long and low. "Two paws down and there's nothing getting done."

Nadya frowned. She'd been able to feed the frog a rock, but there hadn't been anything else for her to fight the frog with, not once it had taken her arm away from her. Still, she couldn't shake the feeling that it was better to be a person who at least *tried* to be a hero, as opposed to someone who didn't try at all, and so rather than dwelling on it, she seized on what seemed like the most important part of what the fox had said: "Community? Are there human people around here?"

Because the fox, while clearly a fox, was also quite clearly a person. People could talk and have opinions about things like frogs and heroes and manners. Animals could be nice—her turtles were animals, and she loved them very much—but they didn't have any of those things. They were just animals. They couldn't be blamed when they did things like scratch or bite or come out of the river and eat your arm. They weren't doing it to be bad or mean. They were doing it to be *animals*.

The fox looked at her thoughtfully before nodding in apparent satisfaction. "There are some, if you'd like me to take you to them. But we'll have to go the rest of the way through the forest to reach them. It's safe, as long as the rain doesn't come before we get there. Still, you might prefer not to."

Nadya couldn't think of a single reason why she wouldn't want to leave the forest and find people, unless . . . "Is it very far to the edge of the wood?" she asked a little anxiously. "My feet are tired, and I'm getting very hungry."

"I'm assuming the frog came out of the River Winsome, since it's the only one around here with frogs as large as you're describing," said the fox, and paused, presumably to give her time to confirm or deny the assumption. Nadya shrugged helplessly. If these rivers had names, she didn't know them. The fox sighed. "If the frog came out of the Winsome, we're halfway between there and the River Wild."

Nadya blinked. "Wouldn't that be the same if the frog came out of the Wild?"

"Yes, but the human people are by the River Wild this time of day, and not the Winsome at all. Plus, I'd rather not go to where there's a frog large enough to think it can make a meal out of a human. I'd be a delicious little snack for a frog like that. No, thank you. If the frog is by the Wild, I'll lead you to the Winsome, but that won't give you people."

"Oh." Nadya frowned. "How do I know which river the frog came from?"

"What else did you see?"

"There were trees along the river's edge, growing in the water, not on the bank, and— Oh! There was another river on the other side, but it was running in the wrong direction. I didn't think rivers could be that close together and run in different directions." Nadya frowned. "It didn't make much sense."

"That was the Winsome, then, and on her other side, the Wicked. Wild is one of the single rivers, and as she doesn't have a sister, she runs a little harsher when the rains come down." The fox hopped off the tree root again. "We'll have to walk as far as you've walked already, and there's no helping that, but I can tell you which berries are safe for humans to eat."

"Thank you, fox," said Nadya, hurrying to straighten up so she could follow the fox. "Um, you asked my name, but I forgot to ask yours. I'm sorry. What would you like me to call you, fox?"

"That's a good way of asking, since I doubt your funny flat face could speak my name if it tried," said the fox, not unkindly. "You can call me Artyom, if you would like."

"Is that your name?"

"Among humans, yes. It means 'beloved of Artemis,' and all foxes are beloved of the Huntress, one way or another."

The fox began to trot deeper into the wood, and Nadya, having no desire to be left alone again, followed.

The ground was no less marshy along the fox's path, but by following his tracks, Nadya found that she could stay out of the worst of the mud. When they reached a bush covered in fat, heavy berries the color of bananas and the shape of raspberries, Artyom sat, flicking his tail.

"These are safe for human stomachs," he said. "I don't care for the taste of them, myself, but hopefully you will, and even if you don't, they'll fill you up from toe to top. Come, eat quickly now, we've a good way yet to go and night will come soon."

Nadya had experience with eating things she didn't care for the taste of. Food was food, and when someone offered it to you, you ate it, because doing otherwise might mean going hungry for longer than you liked. She hastily plucked berries from the bush and conveyed them to her mouth, where she found the flavor to be more pleasant than she'd feared. They were tart and sharp, with a buttery, sugary aftertaste that she generally associated with pancakes or biscuits, not with fruit at all.

Artyom watched with growing impatience, finally rising to wind between her feet as he said, "Most of the humans I've known would fill one hand with berries and pick with the other, and then they could bring berries along with them as they walked. The frog did you a great disservice by eating your arm. We'll have to see if we can get it back again."

Nadya swallowed her mouthful of berries, trying to figure out how to explain prosthetics and birth defects to a fox. Finally, she said, "I don't want the arm back after it's been inside a frog."

"No, I can't imagine that would be particularly pleasant." Artyom sounded displeased. "I suppose there's nothing to be done, then, unless the rivers see fit to provide you with something else."

"I would take a gift from a river," said Nadya.

Artyom gave her what she could only interpret as a pitying look. "Oh, human child. Oh, Nadya. The rivers don't give gifts. They give obligations, and only the unlucky attract that much of their attention."

He began trotting deeper into the wood, apparently judging her to have had enough of the berries for now, and as her stomach was no longer snarling and grumbling, Nadya followed. Her legs were still tired, her feet still hurt, but having a goal and a destination in mind made it easier to keep walking. It was like she could tell her weary body that this would all be over soon and it could rest, and because she had never betrayed it before, it was still willing to listen.

She wasn't sure what would happen if she betrayed it now and tried to make it listen again in the future.

They walked for what felt like at least an hour, until her stomach began to rumble again and she looked to Artyom, silently pleading. The fox huffed, a small sound of annoyance.

"Are human children always this *hungry?*" he asked. "I've been walking the same time as you have, and I haven't run off to chase mice through the weeds even once."

"No," said Nadya, who had seen his jaws snap a few times as something too small for her to see got close enough to catch. She was sure the forest was short a few toads by that point. "But I was walking a long time before you found me crying, and all I've had to eat since the frog were those berries."

"Fine." Artyom sighed, a bigger and deeper sound than his body should have been able to contain. He trotted toward the base of a nearby tree, lowering his nose to the ground, where several large blue mushrooms grew, and sniffed deeply. Then, in a smug tone, he said, "These ones. I've seen humans eat these ones."

Nadya hurried to pluck the largest mushroom, which was easily the size of a hamburger bun, fat and fleshy. "Are all the mushrooms around here safe to eat?"

"Not at all." The fox sat back on his haunches, muzzle hanging open in a silent laugh, as he watched her. "Most of them will kill you just as dead as dead, and then you'll be a treat to fill the belly of the next beast to come along, whether they be fox or boar or bear. Never pick mushrooms without someone who knows them well to guide you. Someone you trust to have your health in mind." He cocked his head, watching her closely. "Now is where we find out if you trust me."

Nadya considered for a moment. Foxes were known to be tricksy creatures, capable of great cunning and deceit. But Artyom had led her clear thus far, and the berries had done her no harm, and she was so hungry.

She brought the mushroom to her mouth and took a large bite of the fleshy cap. It tasted surprisingly like an unbreaded chicken finger, all parts of the bird mashed together, neither dark meat nor white meat, but both of them at once. It was a little bland, but good for all that. She chewed and swallowed before taking another, even bigger bite.

Artyom looked satisfied. "Trust is an important gift, difficult to give and easy to break. But if you trust me, I shall do my best to trust you, and believe you when you speak to me. Come along, Nadezhda. The River Wild is not so far from here."

If they were almost to their destination, there was no need to have shown her the mushroom. Unless it was a test of sorts, to see whether she *was* the kind of human who could be trusted. And she had proven that she was! Feeling oddly proud of herself, Nadya continued following Artyom through the woods, munching on her mushroom as the trees began to thin around them, until they were stepping out of the shadows and onto a wide, grassy strip of land between the forest and another river.

Calling the vast expanse of water "another river" felt somehow dismissive, like she was describing it as something much, much smaller than it was, and not a virtually endless sheet of water rushing from one side of the world to the next at a pace she could never have hoped to match. It was so wide that she could barely see the other side at all, and she couldn't understand how anyone could possibly have mistaken the River Winsome, which was definitely the river she had seen first, for this great sea of tides and currents and rippling rapids.

No frogs were going to come out of *this* river. Even one as large as the frog before would surely have been swept away. Nadya stopped in her tracks, not noticing when the last of the mushroom tumbled from her hand, and simply stared in disbelief at the broad, watery expanse.

"The River Wild, as promised," said Artyom with delight. "And no frogs!"

"No people, either," said Nadya.

"People are mobile things. They'll be along soon enough," said Artyom. "Of course, they might not, if the fishing's done for the day. We shall see, I suppose." He yawned enormously. "Yes, we shall see."

The river rushed. Nadya stood. The river rushed on. The sky roiled gray and black with clouds, as ominous as a Monday afternoon with homework yet undone and all the week's chores looming. Artyom retrieved the remains of Nadya's mushroom and gnawed at them happily.

Time passed. Nadya tired of standing and sat down on the muddy ground. Artyom finished the mushroom and licked his paws clean, before beginning to dart in and out of the weeds, making short work of the mice that made their homes there. The river ran.

Nadya's eyelids were getting heavy and the ground was beginning to look like a pleasant place to nap when Artyom barked, a short, sharply triumphant sound.

"There, you see, you see? I led you correctly!" he cried, and Nadya bolted upright, standing and scanning the horizon, just in time to see what she had taken for a log push its way out of the water, becoming a tall pole. It stayed that way for a moment's time, then continued to emerge from the river, until it was clearly the front of a small boat; the pole was the prow, long and sharp, and the rising pitch behind it was the hull, shaped like a seedpod to cut through the water.

More and more of it emerged, until it seemed the boat must be never-ending, until so much of it was out of the water that she could see a man standing on the deck, a net in his hands, waiting for the moment when gravity would run the right direction. More of the boat emerged. The weight of it was finally more above the river than beneath, and it fell forward, hitting the water with a mighty splash. The man cheered. So did the other four people who had appeared along with the boat.

Nadya blinked.

"Well?" demanded Artyom. "Don't you want to speak with them? They're the reason that I brought you here."

Nadya snapped out of her stillness and ran toward the river, waving her arms above her head.

Artyom laughed and watched her go.

PART III

UNDERWATER

7 PEOPLE OF THE RIVER, PEOPLE OF THE LAKE

THIS WAS WHAT THE PEOPLE on the water saw, as their boat settled into the current and began to drift along the River Wild, carrying them with it: a small, brown-haired girl in muddy clothes, waving her arms in the air as she ran toward them. One arm ended at the elbow, but there was no blood, and it didn't seem to cause her any pain. One of the wood foxes sat on the ground behind her, laughing as she ran.

It was an unusual sight, even for the River Wild, which had seen many an unusual sight in its time. The man at the front of the boat pointed at Nadya, not throwing his net into the water. He said something, but the rushing of the river took it away as all the others turned to watch her running along the bank, their eyes wide and their mouths open in surprise.

Nadya couldn't see, from her place on the shore, how the boat was steered; they seemed to have no oars or pole. But one of the women leaned over the side, long, impossibly dry braids nearly touching the surface of the water, and appeared to say something to the river itself, and the boat began to turn deliberately against the current and move toward the shore.

Nadya stopped running as it became clear that the boat was sailing toward her. She smoothed her hair with her hand and stood up straighter, trying to look less like she had been washed up on a riverbank, chased by a giant frog, and lost in the woods. It was unclear how well she succeeded.

The boat drew closer, and she got a clearer view of the people. There were four of them: two men and two women. The men had short, bushy beards, and the women had long braids, and all of them dressed like they had come out of a picture book about life from centuries before. Their clothing was brightly colored and rich with complicated embroidery, most of it showing fish and waterweeds and ornately shelled turtles.

Nadya relaxed a bit. People who decorated themselves with representations of turtles, but not with actual turtle *shells* the way she'd seen some people do, couldn't be all bad.

The boat drew closer to the shore. The man at the prow leaned toward her, calling, "Hello, girl on the shore! What are you doing here? Did you lose your crew?"

Nadya blinked. "I came through the forest from the River Winsome," she said, pointing behind herself to the trees. "I don't know how I got there."

The man looked at her, expression twisting oddly, and said, "This is not an age of heroes, but doors will open where and when they will. Was there a door?"

Nadya paused. "I thought I saw one in the pond, but that was a shape and shadow, not a door."

"Shadows can be thresholds, under the right conditions. Were you sure?"

"What?"

"When you came through your door, were you sure?"

"Sure of what?" Nadya bit her lip, trying not to let her uncertainty show. "I didn't come through a door. I fell into a shadow in the pond, and then I was on the riverbank. I'm sorry. I don't know how I got here or where 'here' even is, but I'm not sure of *anything.*"

That wasn't quite true. She was sure that her name was Nadya, and that Artyom the fox was her friend, and that these people, with their clothes embroidered in turtles, didn't mean her any harm. Their faces were too open and friendly, and their bearing too carefully unthreatening, for that.

The women exchanged a look as the men frowned. "It certainly *sounds* like you were door-swept," said the man at the prow. "But the warning should have been given, if you were. The warning is always given, to guarantee the swept will be willing. We don't want unwilling children."

Nadya blinked slowly, fear growing in the pit of her stomach like a slow and dreadful weed. "Someone had carved 'be sure' into the back of one of the turtles at the pond," she said, finally. "It was cruel and wrong. Turtles are our friends, and even if they don't like you, they're alive things, not toys! So I was trying to reach the turtle, to be sure it was all right, when I fell into the pond. I was sure the turtle needed me."

The man looked to his companions. One of the women nodded encouragingly and said, "It sounds like she may not have been sure, but Belyyreka was sure enough for both of them. She belongs here."

The man turned back to Nadya. Gentling his expression, he asked, "Child . . . what happened to your arm?"

"I was born without it," said Nadya. "I never needed a second arm to do any of the things I wanted to do, but I had one, made of plastic, from my parents. A big frog came out of the other river and took it." She was getting tired of explaining what had happened to her missing arm. She resolved to start telling glorious lies whenever someone asked her, until they got tired of it and stopped, and let her be.

"Ah," said the man. "This is where we invite you aboard to do the day's fishing with us, and promise to take you to the city when the work is done. Your fox may come as well." He raised his voice, calling, "Fox! Do you want to see the city?"

Artyom yawned enormously and stood, flicking his tail as he trotted over to Nadya. "No, man," he said. "The city is yours and the forest is mine. Human children are yours and have no place with me. I have returned her to you." Then he looked at Nadya, brown eyes grave. "Nadezhda, these people will take you to the human city, where you can better learn the laws of this land. They will not harm you, but I will not be there. If you have need of me, or decide you miss my forest, only call my name, and I will come for you. But be sure before you do, for the river passage is dangerous to my kind, and I cannot come every time you call me."

"I will be sure, Artyom," said Nadya solemnly. The small fox flicked his tail and raced away, a tawny streak heading into the shadows of the trees. Nadya watched him go, and when he was no longer in sight, turned back to the boat, where the man was holding out his hand.

After a moment's hesitation she took it, and he helped her step over the side, into the boat, which rocked a little but was otherwise surprisingly stable. Once inside, she could see that there were low benches built into the sides, places for the people to sit, and piles of nets and baskets.

"Inna, Galina, let Vasyl know we're ready to resume," said the man to the two women. They nodded in unison and moved to the side of the boat, leaning over together and whispering to the water. The boat, slowly, backed away from the shore and turned back toward the center of the river. Nadya blinked, wide-eyed and wondering.

"Is the boat alive?" she asked. "Are you telling it what you want of it?"

The shorter of the two women laughed. "No, not at all," she said. "Vasyl is my friend. He chose me when he was smaller, and now he takes me as I ask him. But he is very large and sometimes I can be hard to hear, and so my sister's voice aids my own."

"Oh," said Nadya, confused.

"It will all make sense soon," promised the woman. She picked up a net and moved toward the side of the boat, her sister moving with her. The two men picked up nets as well. The boat steering on its own accord meant that none of them needed to spend their time steering, and they could all toss their nets over the side.

As they did, they began to sing. Nadya sat down on one of the low benches and listened, eyes drifting shut. The words were unfamiliar, but the tune felt like something she had known in childhood, something so familiar that she didn't need to remember it to know it. The fishers sang and the boat sailed and Nadya listened.

And then, somewhere in the middle of the song, Nadya slept.

She woke to the boat shaking all around her, and a floor covered in fish. Most of them were silvery, but some were brown, or banded in pink and blue scales, like delicate pieces of art. Most were dead. A few flopped weakly, unable to launch themselves over the sides from where they were. The smell was surprisingly mild and distant, not as overpowering as she would have expected from dead, raw fish.

The pile nearest Nadya shifted positions. She sat up a little straighter, glancing around. The people who had been doing the fishing were chatting among themselves, packing their nets away. They weren't singing anymore, or paying the slightest bit of attention to her. They didn't seem bothered by the way the boat was shaking, and so she decided that she wouldn't be either, and focused on the moving pile of fish.

They weren't flopping or trying to breathe. They were

just . . . sliding, like something was pushing its way up from beneath them. She frowned and leaned closer, then gasped as a small, beaked head pushed its way to the surface and looked at her with round yellow eyes.

"Hello, turtle," she said, delighted by the appearance of such a familiar friend. It continued looking at her, not pulling away or trying to hide under the fish. "Did they sweep you up by mistake? Careless of them. Do you want help back into the river?"

The turtle cocked its head, seeming to consider, before replying serenely, "No. I am here because I would prefer to be here, and your help is not required."

The fox talking had been like something out of a story. Of course a fox with no fear, in the middle of a flooded forest, would talk! More unusual if it *didn't*. But a turtle in a fishing boat is not the same as a fox in a forest, and so Nadya stared for a long moment before she squeaked, "Can all turtles talk?"

"All turtles in Belyyreka can," said the turtle. "I don't know about the turtles on the other side of your door, Drowned Girl, but *proper* turtles understand *proper* grammar and how to use it."

"I'm not drowned," protested Nadya. "Drowned people are dead people or . . . or rusalki, and I'm not either of those things."

"As you say," grumbled the turtle, and vanished back under the mountain of fish. Nadya looked up, frowning, and saw that the prow of the ship was dipping down, down, ever farther down, until it broke the surface of the water.

Once there, it kept going. The fish began to slide, and the people were ready with their nets, throwing them over their catch, keeping it from going tumbling out into the river as the boat tipped more and more. Nadya grabbed her seat, finding small handholds under the edge, places she could hook her fingers and hold tightly on, keeping herself from falling. She shrieked as the boat stood on end, half in the water and half out, and began sinking rapidly, taking them all with it.

At the last moment, she thought to take a deep breath and hold it, so that when they slid beneath the surface of the water, she didn't start to choke at once.

The boat kept going downward, not quite in a straight line, but leveling out. The fishers released their nets, which floated up a few inches before the weights on them caught and held them down. Then they began to sing again.

Their song, which had been bright and compelling above the water, was almost hypnotic here, beneath the water. It rose and fell with the currents around them, ebbing and eddying. Nadya didn't understand how she could hear it so clearly, or how it could be so bright beneath the surface of the river, as bright, almost, as sunlight. Brighter even than the cloudy land above.

It wasn't until they reached the chorus that she realized her mouth was hanging open and she was breathing in her shock, filling her lungs with river water that didn't feel like water at all, but like the air on a misty morning, thick and cool, yes; still breathable. She coughed, choking just a little, and clutched her throat.

Inna turned to look at her, breaking off from the song and moving closer. "It's all right, Nadya," she said. "Breathe if you can breathe. The river won't hold you responsible for taking a part of it into yourself."

Nadya stared at her. "Are you . . . are you rusalki?" she asked, voice a squeak.

"No," said Inna. "We are the people of Belyyreka, and you are one of us, door-swept and Drowned. The foxes of the forest and the turtles of the tides talk to you, and you hear them clearly. You are more sure than ever you knew or understood, and we are so delighted to be the ones lucky enough to be welcoming you home."

She smiled, then, the sweet, melting smile of a new mother looking at a child in the orphanage, a child who had just, through the mysterious alchemy of paperwork, become her own. Nadya glanced around. The other three were still singing, and in the distance she could see more boats like theirs descending through the bright water toward the river bottom. She gasped.

The shape of the boats was as she had supposed when seen from above, but each of them was tethered, with a series of straps and ropes, to the back of a turtle larger than any she had ever seen before. She looked toward the front of their boat, resisting the urge to rush forward and check.

Inna smiled. "Yes, Vasyl is my friend. He chose me when I was just a Drowned Girl, like you. He was larger than our little one here." She indicated the turtle still rummaging through their fish. "This one is still too small, I think, to want to bond himself to a human, however appealing. But there are other turtles at the shipyard who will be delighted to meet you, I think, and glad to have the opportunity. Drowned and unchosen are rare enough in a year without need of heroes that there's little chance you'll go without."

"Don't get the child's hopes up before they've seen her," called Galina. "Not all Drowned Girls find their companions."

"Don't mind my sister," said Inna. "She's Belyyreka-born, and needed no anchor to be sure she'd stay where the proper people are. So no one chose her, and now she sails with me, to aid my crew in their catches, and has no companion of her own."

Nadya didn't know what to make of that, or of the way Galina laughed and turned to poke her tongue out at Inna, leaving them both giggling like much younger girls. So she looked to the first man she'd met, whose name she still didn't know, and begged for an explanation with her eyes.

He took some pity on her, because he came closer and sat on the nearest low bench, saying, "This is a new place, and like all new places, it will have new rules. We're glad to have you, and we'll do our best not to confuse you *too* badly."

"This is . . . Belyyreka?" Nadya's tongue stumbled over the new word, although not as badly as she might have stumbled over something that felt less Russian and thus less familiar. It was like a word she'd heard before, whispered in dreams, calling her to find it. The word felt like coming home.

"Yes," said the man. "This is Belyyreka, and I am Borya, and I, like Inna, like you, was brought here by a door when I was very young. Only the very young are capable of uncomplicated surety, you see, and so the doors seek them when they are lost and need to come home. Sometimes people, like tales, begin where they do not belong. Do you understand?"

"Yes," lied Nadya, who was well acquainted with adults asking questions when they already knew which answer they wanted to receive.

Borya looked at her, frowning like he didn't quite believe her. Then he nodded and said, "Those who are born here, like Inna's sister and my brother, they belong to Belyyreka. The only doors that come for them will be the ones who recognize that this is not their home. But those who are brought here, they need something to tie them to the great lake, or their original homes may call them back, whether they wish to go or no."

Nadya blinked, very slowly. "So are you from Colorado?" she asked.

Borya laughed. "No," he said. "I was born in a city of towers, by an ocean I hope never to see again. The water was salt and bitterness and it wanted nothing of the people who lived on the land. The sea teemed with merfolk, and they would never forgive us for the crimes we had committed against them when our world was much younger. The city was like a coat six sizes too big for me, and it never fit, and I could never be the person I was expected to become. So when a door appeared where no door belonged, I went through, and I never looked back."

Inna looked away from the side of the boat and said, "I came from a city called Manhattan, where my parents had seven children and no time for any of us, but always time for making more children. I was always hungry and always lonely and always serving as a mother for the children younger than myself, even though I was scarce a child myself. I fell into the harbor one day while I was begging for bread, and I found myself washed up on the banks of the River Wild, where a fishing boat brought me in as part of their day's catch."

"Even as we're doing now, with you," said Galina amiably. "Drowned Girls and Drowned Boys go to the harbormaster, who knows all the answers to all the questions, and doesn't think any of them are foolish in the slightest."

That was a good thing for Nadya to hear. She had already had more than her share of being looked at pityingly by adults for asking questions that seemed perfectly reasonable and important to her, but turned out to be things that "everyone knew" and thus never needed to ask about. She liked the idea of no questions being seen as foolish, even if they were questions about the things that "everyone knew." She liked that idea a lot.

"How many of us are there?" asked Nadya eagerly. It seemed there must be a great many, if two out of the first four people she'd met had come from other worlds, through doors, like she had.

"Quite a few," said Borya. "More than there used to be, but not as many as some worlds have. The world I came from knew about the doors, and knew that they ran in both directions, and when children came through, we would try our best to send them back, lest their parents be sad at losing them, although the merfolk didn't do the same; for them, when children washed up on their tides, those children were gifts of the storm, and they were kept and cosseted."

"I think we came from the same world, Nadya," said Inna. "At least, the name of Colorado is familiar to me, and I've never heard of two worlds so close together that they named things the same. Our world only knows the doors in stories and cautionary tales, and few people travel there from elsewhere."

"Can they follow me here?" asked Nadya. "Carl and— My parents, can they find me?"

"No," said Inna, with careful sorrow in her voice, and Nadya found that she was relieved.

They weren't cruel to her, Carl and Pansy, were even kind in their slightly distant way, but she didn't love them, and she knew they didn't love her. What was love, anyway? Was it a form of possession? She had loved Maksim, very much, and that was why she had sent him away to a home where he could be happy and well cared for, all the days of his life. She liked to think that he had been happy with her, even as she had been happy at the orphanage, but she knew he'd be better off with a home of his own, where he never had to be hidden away to keep inspectors from seeing him and rejecting him as a wild animal, where the food was always fresh and the water always clean.

By that standard, the matrons must have loved her, or they wouldn't have sent her away to America. But she knew they hadn't. It wasn't hurtful knowledge: her hair was brown, her right arm ended at the elbow, the matrons never loved her. Also by that standard, Carl and Pansy loved her more than anything, because they'd given her so many wonderful things, shoes like pillows and food so delicious that sometimes it didn't seem real.

But things weren't love. They didn't look to her the way some of the smaller children at the orphanage had, eyes soft and faces full of light. They looked at each other that way, if rarely, and the other parents at her school looked at their children that way, but Carl and Pansy didn't, because they didn't love her. Things weren't love, and she was a thing to them, a thing that required many other things to be content, but not entirely a person.

It wasn't like that for the other adopted children in her school, whose parents looked at them with love, who didn't know what it was to be a thing, but it was like that for her. Sometimes a thing could be one thing for one person and another thing for someone else. Something like the way rivers couldn't be breathed anywhere else she'd ever been, and turtles couldn't talk, but here, both those things were possible.

"I'm glad," said Nadya. "I didn't like the big frog who came to eat me, but everything else has been very good, and I think I want to stay in Belyyreka."

Vasyl swam on, and the boat moved with him, pulled along

by ropes and straps. The fishers moved around their catch, layering more nets, securing what they'd gathered, pausing only to free the small turtle before they tied it entirely down. As soon as Galina lifted him from the pile of fish, he swam upward from her hand, stubby legs thrashing against the water that seemed so much like air to Nadya but was clearly still water for him.

"Goodbye, Drowned Girl," said the turtle to her, politely enough. He swam a circle around her head and then he was gone, shooting away into the current.

"Goodbye," called Nadya. The boat sank lower, other boats coming closer, so she could see the majestic size of the turtles that towed them. Some were easily as large as cars, their shells broader than the span of a grown man's arms. Others were smaller, and their boats were smaller as well, little more than coracle shells with a single fisher waving to their peers from the boat's edge. All the turtles swam with single-minded purpose toward the same destination in the city below.

Nadya moved to the boat's edge and leaned as far out as she dared, peering down at the bottom of the river.

They were moving toward a city.

It was made of stone, piled high and towering, gray and black and white and brown, slick and clean. Waterweeds grew up through the foundations, and a web of what looked like docks spread out in layers around each of the tallest buildings. It etched a lacy pattern in the water, impossibly delicate, too extended to have been possible without the water holding it up from all sides. There was something concretely natural about it, like even the parts that had been constructed had been built on the bones of what the river made on its own.

Nadya looked up. The surface of the water was so far above them now that it looked exactly like the sky.

Borya smiled at her. "This is why we need the turtles," he said. "They change the shape of the distance. It compresses for them, because the rivers love them as the great lake loves us."

"What?"

"The harbormaster will explain it all, I promise." Borya looked to Inna. "Sing us home."

"Of course." Inna leaned over the side again. This time, the song she started was faster and jauntier, filled with interior rhymes that set an almost-galloping rhythm. The other fishers joined in, and Nadya found herself wishing she knew the words, that she might do the same.

Oh! to be a fisher on and under this great river! To sail a ship on turtle-back and see the world from both sides of the water! It would be a glorious thing indeed! The things they had said were fragmented and strange, but still, they stuck with her, making her think that perhaps this could be her future—a turtle for a companion, like Inna, and a good ship beneath her, carrying her to whatever destinations she desired. She didn't yet know this place or these people well enough to know whether she wanted to stay there forever, but she didn't find the idea unattractive in the shape it had to offer her.

Yes. She could be happy here.

Vasyl changed the angle of his swimming, going from a straight line to a spiral, gently winding his way toward the nearest of those tall, lace-wrapped towers. It drew closer with daunting speed, until the lacy docks looked less like decoration and more like the functional structures they were, bustling with people carting baskets of fish and strange vegetables and piles of nets, lined with little stalls and individual docking posts. The expected boats were tied up there, with space beside them for their turtles, who ate out of vast troughs of fish and greenery, occasionally lifting their massive heads to converse with the people passing by.

It looked very much like paradise to Nadya. She bounced in place, fighting the urge to jump off the boat and swim to the dock. Only the fact that water seemed to turn to air without warning here, and she didn't really know how to swim, kept her where she was. Inna smiled indulgently.

"I felt the same way when I first saw Belyyreka," she said. "Patience, child. You're home now. The Drowned are never cast aside."

Nadya tamped down her excitement as they pulled up to the dock, and Borya hopped out, tying up the boat before releasing Vasyl from his bonds, murmuring thanks to the great turtle as he swam up from beneath them and moved into position at his trough. Nadya swallowed. He was so *big*, bigger than any turtle she'd ever imagined could exist in the entire world. And he was beautiful, dark green with yellow streaks down the sides of his head, and big orange eyes that made her think fall must be the sweetest season.

"H-hello," she said, as politely as she could manage.

Those big orange eyes fixed on her. "Hello, Drowned Girl," said the turtle Vasyl. "Have you had a grand adventure?"

"I don't think so," said Nadya. "I had a journey, but I didn't have an adventure, not really. I didn't save anything important or find anything that had been lost."

"You saved yourself," said Vasyl. "I would think that is the most important adventure of all."

Nadya, who had never thought of it that way, said nothing, only sat in weighted silence as the turtle continued, "And you found Belyyreka, the Land Beneath the Lake, which many say has been lost forever."

"There's no lake," protested Nadya. "I didn't see any lake at all. I fell into a pond and washed up in a river. Those aren't the same as lakes."

"But you *did* see the lake, if you looked up at all," said Vasyl. "The surface of it stretches above the clouds, and the bravest of us can swim that high if they are quick, if they are clever and strong, if they desire to know what dry air tastes like in their throats. This whole land is a Drowned Land, and you are a Drowned Girl, for nothing breathes the air in Belyyreka, only different weights of water."

Nadya blinked at the turtle, and when Borya came to help her out of the boat, she went without question or complaint, letting him lead her along the dock, away from the boat. Only as they were approaching a long, low building with lights burning in the windows—and how could anything burn there, at the bottom of a river? How could any of this be possible?—did she look at him and ask, "Are we really all drowned here?"

"Of course," he said, voice soft. "What else would we be?"

Straightening, he yelled, "Harbormaster! A door-swept daughter for your custodianship!"

The door opened. A broad, smiling man with a beard like a bush appeared, blocking most of the light.

He gestured, and Nadya went inside.

8 THE LAND BENEATH THE LAKE

THE HARBORMASTER'S NAME was Ivan, which seemed like the best and most serviceable of names to Nadya, who allowed herself to be led into his small, cozy study, with its chairs upholstered in buttery leather and candles burning all around the edges of the room. He saw her frowning at the fire like it was entirely incomprehensible, and he smiled.

"Let me guess; you don't understand how fire can burn beneath the surface of a river?"

"I don't understand how a river can run under a lake, or how we can breathe and not die. We don't have gills like fish do; we shouldn't be able to survive here, unless someone has been lying to me." Nadya fixed him with a hard gaze. "If I've been underwater since I fell into the pond, I should be as dead as any victim of the rusalki by now. How is this happening?"

"At least you aren't trying to claim it's not," said the harbormaster, and took a seat in one of the chairs, gesturing for her to do the same. "Some of the door-swept begin by denying everything that's happening around them, claiming that because it doesn't fit the world as they understand it to work, it can't be true. That gets tiresome fairly quickly."

"A giant frog came out of the river and ate my arm," said Nadya. "I don't think pretending it didn't happen would do me any good, and if that happened, then everything else is happening, too." Talking foxes and lakes in the sky and giant turtles and all.

And admittedly, she really *wanted* the giant turtles to be happening. She wanted it more than she'd ever wanted almost anything.

The harbormaster nodded. "Do all children have detachable arms where you come from?"

"No. It was a prosthetic—a tool made to look like an arm, to fill the gap where people thought an arm was meant to be." Nadya waved the stump of her right arm in his direction, making sure he saw it. "I was born without one."

"You seem to be doing quite well for all of that."

Nadya shrugged. "I never had that arm. I never missed it. When the people I lived with bought me the prosthetic, they said I had to wear it, and so I did, but that didn't make it something I needed to have to be happy. I wouldn't have minded as much if they'd *asked* me, but they never did."

"That arm probably saved your life from the frog. Do frogs get big enough to eat little girls in the world you come from?"

Nadya shook her head.

"Well, then, we'll begin there. This is Belyyreka, the Land Beneath the Lake. It's also been called the Land of a Million Rivers, although I suppose there are rather more than a million, if you were to count them all. That's the first thing new arrivals have to understand: water has weight, and different water has different weight. The water of the lake is very light, almost like the substance some people call air. You can breathe it and never notice, but you're still breathing water, and you're still Drowned. The water in the rivers is heavier, which means it falls to the bottom of the lake and runs there, heading for the great spouts that will drive it back up into the clouds, where it can fall again. Water loves falling. Do you understand?"

Nadya pictured great columns of water climbing into the sky like the legs on a table, and nodded.

"Even the water in the rivers is lighter than the water in the world you come from, and our water is the lightest anyone has ever heard of, which is why you can breathe it and don't need air. But all of us are Drowned, and are never to be dry again, and quite happily so. You wouldn't be here if you didn't belong here. The doors choose." His last words sounded almost reverent.

Nadya frowned. "Inna, on the boat, said something very much like that. She seems to think the doors are normal things that people should have heard of. But I've never heard of a door that takes you under a lake to where the water is air and foxes can talk. I think someone would have said something. I'm not even certain I went through a door at all. There was a shape in the weeds that might have been a door, if you looked at it the right way, but might not have been a door at all. And then I fell through it."

"And you wound up here, so it was a door, and had something different on its other side." The harbormaster's smile was an encouragement and a congratulations. "Not every world the doors touch admits their existence. We do, here, because how else would we explain children who panic when their heads are pulled underwater? If you were Belyyreka-born, none of this would be necessary. You would know how the world has always worked, and expect it to continue along its familiar tracks."

"One of the women on my boat, she spoke to the turtle who steered us. Called him her companion. And said she had been chosen when she was just a Drowned Girl. What did she mean?"

"Ah. Well, the Drowned Children who come here from elsewhere, they have no bonds to Belyyreka when they first arrive. No families to keep them, no homes to call their own.

And so the great turtles who live here with us at the bottom of the lake have agreed to shepherd them, when they have the numbers to do so. They adopt the Drowned, become their families—even more than the Belyyrekans who sometimes volunteer the same role, as human children need human hands and human beds to keep them safe and comfortable, but who can never replace the families the children left behind. And then they stay together, and we hope the Drowned will be happy here. Happy enough to be sure."

"What does that mean?"

"You must be sure you have nothing binding you to the place where you are in order to pass through a door. If you had been less confident that you could go without leaving a hole behind, then falling into your waterweeds would have resulted in a splash, not a passage. But children can be sure of something one second and questioning the validity of it the next. If we don't make sure this is your home, you might lose your certainty, and the doors might come to take you back."

Sudden fear gripped Nadya, strong enough that she sat bolt upright in the chair and said, "No. I don't want to go back there."

"Ah." The harbormaster didn't look surprised. "The lost and the lonely, those are the ones who find their way to us when we have no call for heroes. The lost and the lonely. We find them, and we give them purpose, and we keep them as well as we can, and as long as they are sure of us, they stay. I hope you will be one of those who stays."

Nadya sagged, fear flagging and taking what remained of her energy with it. "When can I meet the turtles?"

"In the morning. You're exhausted, child, and you deserve the chance to sleep your fears away."

Part of Nadya knew this was a dream, and that to sleep in

dreams was to wake in the real world. But the greater part of her knew that it didn't matter; she was tired and sore and still distantly hungry. Still, one question remained . . .

"How *do* you have candles here?"

"Our water is light, but our fire is hot," said the harbormaster. "It can burn even in very dark places. Rest, and know that you are safe."

Nadya's eyes could barely stay open. She yawned enormously, snuggling into the corner of the chair, and everything dropped away but dreaming.

When she woke, it was a slow process, like swimming up from the bottom of a deep pond. She kept her eyes closed, measuring her breathing, trying to listen to the room around her. Something had been spread across her body, a blanket or coat; she was warm and weighted down. She might be in the harbormaster's chair in Belyyreka, or she might be asleep in the back of the car, under Carl's jacket in the parking lot again.

A soft voice intruded on the edge of her awareness, singing a rolling, gentle song that wasn't quite a lullaby but was something closer to a mourning song. The harbormaster said jovially, "Come in, Inna. Oh, biscuits? What a lovely start to the day!"

"The girl," said Inna. "Has anyone yet inquired for her?"

"Are you so ready, then, to start a family?" The question was lightly asked, but Nadya recognized the tone. It was the tone the matrons had taken on the rare occasions when someone they thought was too young showed up to ask about the children in their care.

"I have good work on the fishing boats, and a sister who loves me and has a husband and two children of her own, but I have no wish to marry," said Inna. "We spoke on the boat,

Nadya and I, and she sounds as if she comes from the same world I did, which would make my home less confusing to her. I know the questions she's likely to ask, and what the best answers are to be honest and not overwhelming. Adaptation to Belyyreka can be hard for a new Drowned Girl. I'd like it to be easier for her than it was for me, if it can."

"Then you may speak with her when she wakes, although I believe she's more interested in talking to the turtles than she is in seeking a human guardian."

Inna laughed. "I wasn't looking for a new human family when I landed here. It's no surprise that she's not either."

Nadya opened her eyes, finally confident that she wasn't dreaming but would in fact find herself looking out on the harbormaster's office. He and Inna were seated in chairs across from the one where she had fallen asleep; it was his jacket laid across her. She sat up, grabbing the jacket to keep it from falling to the floor, and he turned toward the motion, smiling warmly.

"I thought you might be awake," he said. "Inna has offered you a place in her home, if you wish to take it. She is unmarried, but her sister and her sister's husband also live with her, and you would not be—"

"I would be happy to," blurted Nadya. Inna smiled at her, and Nadya smiled back, suddenly shy. "But if we find we like each other less than we hope . . ."

"You can always return here," the harbormaster reassured her. "Our goal is happiness for the Drowned, not misery."

"Then it sounds perfect." Nadya stood, laying the coat on the chair. Then she winced. "But I would like to see your restroom first, if I could, please."

The harbormaster laughed. Nadya kept smiling, the faintly mortified smile of a child being forced to discuss such things in front of unfamiliar adults, and he directed her out of his office and down the hall to the bathroom, which, she was relieved to see, was more modern than the candlelit office would have implied; the plumbing was all bronze and polished wood, no ceramic, but when she turned the tap, hot water came out. How that could be possible when they were already under the surface of a river, she didn't know and didn't want to ask. The harbormaster would probably just tell her another story about some water being heavier than other water, and her head was still spinning from the night before.

She washed up, splashing water over her face with her hand, and looked at herself for a moment in the mirror before leaving the room and heading back toward the harbormaster's office, stepping as lightly as she could to keep her approach from being overheard. As she drew closer, she slowed, listening as closely as she could.

"She's still new here," the harbormaster was saying. "If she changes her mind, if it's all too much—you mustn't get too attached, Inna, she could be called back to the world of her birth at any time."

"I do understand how the doors work, Ivan," said Inna, almost chidingly. "I'll keep her as safe as I'm allowed, and encourage her to find as much danger as she needs, and she'll serve Belyyreka well."

"And the missing arm—"

"Is not a flaw. If she wants to replace it with something to help her grasp and steer, she can, and if not, she will still be entire and intact as she is. She's perfect, Ivan. Perfect for Belyyreka, and perfect for me."

Nadya smiled and stepped back into the office. "I hear biscuits?" she said hopefully.

They were American biscuits, close to the syrniki Nadya

remembered from home, sweet and flaky with currants and unfamiliar nuts tucked between the layers like little surprises of taste and texture. She took a bite, chewed, swallowed, and turned wide eyes toward Inna. "You are Russian?" she asked, with some surprise.

"My grandparents were," said Inna. "They moved to America to make a better life for their children, and when I was a little younger than you are now, my nana taught me to bake. Many things here will be familiar, Nadya, and many will be strange. I think the doors understand us well enough to know how much strangeness each of our hearts can handle, and they choose their children accordingly. Many of the people you'll find here who came from our first world have Russia in their roots."

That explained the names, and the comfortable shape of things. Nadya nodded, swallowing her mouthful of syrniki, and said, "I still want to meet the turtles, but I'm willing to go with you now."

And Inna smiled.

ADOPTION—IF THAT WAS what this was—worked very differently here than it did back in Russia. No papers were signed, no money changed hands, unless biscuits were money here; Inna simply handed the rest of the plate to the harbormaster, took Nadya by the hand, and said, "Come on now, we're going home," before leading her out of the office and onto the dock.

Rather than turning to head deeper into the city then, she began walking out along one of the long fronds of planked wood, pulling Nadya with her. Nadya walked in obedient quiet for a few minutes, then tilted her head up and asked, "Where are we going?"

"Home, eventually," said Inna. "But I remember how overwhelming all of this was when it began for me, and I thought you might like something to anchor yourself by before we go any further. I know you're taking a very large leap of faith by trusting me. I want to prove I *can* be trusted."

Nadya didn't say anything. The turtles trusted Inna, and still weary and overwhelmed as she was, she trusted the turtles. She always had. She couldn't say precisely why, and she didn't feel like she should have to. Some people trusted other people, some people trusted religion or people on the news, and she trusted turtles. It was just one more way a person could be made differently.

They walked along the long wooden dock to another building, this one made of paler wood, with windows shaped like a turtle's shell. Inna led Nadya inside, to where a woman sat behind a tall counter. "Clear currents, Anna," said Inna.

The woman—Anna—looked up and smiled. "Clear currents, Inna," she said. "Come for Vasyl already?"

"No. I have a new charge." She indicated Nadya. "She's been door-swept, and she wants to meet the young turtles. Perhaps one of them will care for her company."

"Welcome to Belyyreka," said Anna, turning her smile on Nadya. "Most of the fishing boats have gone for the day. You're welcome, both of you."

Inna nodded and led Nadya through a small door at the back of the room, into a narrow hall that smelt of wood rot and wet in a way that nothing else had so far. They walked along that hall to a room that opened up like a cavern, and in the center of it was a vast pool of heavier water, liquid and shimmering, and in the pool . . .

Oh, in the pool were the turtles. Dozens upon dozens of turtles, more turtles than Nadya had ever dreamt. Some were the size of Vasyl, drifting lazily toward the bottom of the water or lounging on the slope that filled one entire end of the pool. Others were much, much smaller, ranging in size from turtles small enough to fit in her palm to roughly as big as a large serving platter. It was the smaller turtles who swarmed the water's edge where they were standing, stretching their heads out of the water and calling greetings in high, piping voices, like the tuning of a vast orchestra made entirely of flutes. Inna released Nadya's hand and knelt, murmuring greetings to the turtles.

There were so many that Nadya was overwhelmed, not sure how she was supposed to respond or answer. She drifted a few feet away, suddenly shy.

A single head, belonging to a turtle about two feet across, poked out of the water and looked at her. "Hello," said the turtle. "You smell of other waters."

"I'm a Drowned Girl," said Nadya. "I just got here from Colorado."

"So they brought you to meet the hopeful straightaway? Oh, they must want to keep you." The turtle sounded amused. "Shouldn't you be making nice to convince one of the fawning frenzy to choose you as their bosom companion?"

"Maybe I want you to choose me," said Nadya, feeling a little bolder.

The turtle looked at her gravely. "Do you?"

"I don't know yet. We just met. I don't even know your name."

"My name is Burian," said the turtle. "And you don't want me, even if you think I do."

Nadya blinked. "Why don't I?"

"I'm too big to live comfortably in a human house for long; I'd have to leave you far too soon. But I'm too small to pull a boat for years yet, if I ever can. Look." He rose higher out of the water, showing her the jagged crack that ran across his shell, showing where it had been broken and healed. "I'll never be able to haul as much as the others can."

Nadya sat down, letting her feet dangle into the heavier water, and smiled at the turtle. "What if I don't want to run a boat?" she asked. "Would I want you to choose me then?"

PART IV

TIME IS A RIVER

9 A CHILD GROWS UP

TIME IS A RIVER, or so they say in almost every world where time runs in a linear fashion and not in awkward, disconnected pools of causality that may or may not remain the same from day to day: time is a river, and like all rivers, it runs where it wishes, and cannot be stopped. Our time together is never as long as we would like, and so we must now move downstream perhaps more quickly than we would like. It is a pleasant thing, to linger in currents clean and clear, where we know nothing will hurt us. Sometimes, though, the fishing is better where the water moves more quickly. Sometimes, we must move on.

Burian did indeed choose Nadya, and none was more delighted by this pairing than Anna, who had feared Burian would never find a person of his own. Having people was not a necessity to the turtles of Belyyreka, but they were social creatures who enjoyed having someone to call their own that they could spend time with and work with as they reached their adult sizes. Their window of "large enough to feel safe leaving the company of their mothers, but small enough to fit through human doors and windows" was brief enough that they hurried to find their people while they could. It was not unheard-of for smaller turtles to choose infants, or older ones to meet unpartnered adults, but it was rare. Rare indeed.

Turtles were strong enough to swim in the thinnest water, which looked like flying to Nadya but made the turtles essential for moving between the levels of the lake, from the deepest water all the way up to where the heavy rivers ran. To befriend a turtle was to know true freedom, and Nadya could imagine nothing better.

Inna took Nadya into her home, which was small and warm and filled with laughter. The two children already there were both younger than Nadya, a sticky six and a curious four, and she found them a comfort and a delight, as well as a convenience, as by sitting in the room while they had their lessons, she could quietly learn the things people assumed a child her age would already know. Inna taught her to bake syrniki, and how to dry the round green berries that served them as currants, lacking either true currants or grapes to wither for sultanas.

And Nadya grew. She grew by leaps and bounds, her belly full enough to build her body and her heart full enough to build everything else about her. She grew tall and straight and stronger than anyone had ever asked her to be, joining Galina and Inna on the fishing boat more days than not, learning the fishing songs and how to properly tie and cast a net. The knots that seemed too complex to be performed with one hand could often be accomplished through the addition of a stick held between her knees, to pull the strands taut while she worked. No one would claim Nadya's lack of a hand made things easier for her, but it certainly didn't have to make them harder.

While Nadya was growing, Burian was doing the same, and one day he could no longer fit through the window of what had become her bedroom but had to hover outside, legs kicking against the mild current of the thin water. Nadya began spending more of her free time outside with him, and the two became hellions, racing from place to place along the docks, laughter bright as pearls in the thin water. They weren't the only young ones running wild; running wild was a time-honored tradition in Belyyreka, for those old enough to be restless but too young to serve the city in more formal ways. Perhaps it would have been better if they were, as one day their racing brought them into a new part of the city, where the docks were narrower and closer together, and the streets were layered in a pattern neither of them recognized.

Nadya slowed, then stopped, trying to make sense of everything around them. Burian swam a slow circle around her head, doing much the same. "We should go back," he said. "We've gone farther than we normally do."

Nadya was reasonably fearless, but when Burian got nervous, she knew enough to do the same. She started to turn, to head back, and stopped at the sight of a boy standing directly in her path.

He was taller than her, broader in the shoulders, if not much older; he wore the simple clothes she had come to associate with the fishing families, cut so as not to risk snagging on nets or lines, dyed in berry-bright colors. Most of them were rich with embroidery, but not his. That only held her attention for a moment before the light glinting off the fishing hook in his right hand caught her eye, and held it.

"You're not so special," said the boy. "You're just another swept-away, and there's nothing special about you."

Nadya, who had never seen the boy before, blinked, trying to figure out where the hostility in his voice had come from. It seemed too big for him to be talking about her or Burian. He had to be talking about someone else. Only she'd heard the term "swept-away" before, used by the older fishers who thought she had no place on the boats, that a child who could be careless enough to fall through one door must inevitably fall through another and leave them short-handed during a storm, unable to steer or sing loud enough for their turtle to hear.

Every boat had a turtle. Only they could swim against the strong currents at the top of River Wild, swim hard enough and fast enough to pull the boats up and onto the surface of the river. The turtles could keep swimming from there if they so chose, all the way to the top of the lake, but few of them did so. Humans couldn't swim in water that thin, and would fall if their boat shook even a little. It seemed better not to risk their partners so.

Nadya took a step backward. The boy took a step forward, and so the distance between them stayed the same.

"Nasty little swept-away," he muttered. "Coming here and taking up space that belongs to Belyyreka. Someone else's stomach goes empty so yours can be full." And he lunged, swinging his hook at her. It was a long, wicked thing, meant to puncture and pull, meant to *hurt*.

Nadya jumped away, and her heels hit the edge of the dock, and she fell.

She still didn't understand the nature of water in Belyyreka, and she wasn't sure anyone else did, either. Some water was thin enough to breathe, and other water wasn't. The water of the rivers was breathable when you were *under* the surface, but not when you were *above* the surface. Most of the adults were dreadfully incurious about the inconsistent nature of the water, seeming to accept it as just the way the world worked, perhaps because they'd been accustomed to it for too long.

Nadya, however, was not accustomed to it. Nadya had been studying it as much as she could, between fishing expeditions and classes and spending time with Burian. She knew even before her feet left the dock that she was going to be in trouble. The water here was thin enough to breathe, and that meant that while it would *slow* a human, it wouldn't *stop* her. She was denser than the water, and would keep falling until she hit either heavier water or the bottom, which was so far below her that she would surely be hurt, if not outright killed. She flailed, grabbing the edge of the dock with her one hand, and tried to pull herself back up.

She failed. Her arm was strong, but not strong enough to hoist the full weight of her body onto the platform. Panting, Nadya dangled.

The boy, who had looked a little frightened when she first fell, like this hadn't been what he intended, resumed his expression of smug bravado and crouched down, smirking at her. "Aw, little swept-away isn't strong enough to save herself? Poor thing. I'll help you."

He reached for her hand. Nadya bared her teeth. "If you touch me, I'll gut you first chance I get," she snarled. He pulled back, looking startled, an expression which only grew as Burian slammed into him from behind and sent him toppling over the edge.

Turtles should not push children off of high walkways, although Burian might be forgiven under the circumstances. But the boy, falling, panicked even as Nadya had done, and grabbed hold of her ankle before he could fall too far. The addition of his weight to her own yanked her downward, and she almost lost her grip on the dock. "Burian!" she shouted.

"Nadya, what can I do? What can I do?"

"Go get help!"

There wasn't anything else the stranger boy could do to hurt her, not when he was already dangling from her ankle and weighing her down. Burian circled her once, anxiously, and shot off toward the harbormaster's office, where he could hopefully find and return with Ivan. The big man would happily shut down any mischief on his docks.

Realizing where the big turtle was going, the boy yelped and began trying to scramble up the length of Nadya's body, nearly dislodging her in the process. "Hey!" she snapped. "Stop, or we're *both* going to fall."

He stopped and just held on.

"Why were you being such a jerk to me, anyway? I don't even know you, but you pushed me off the dock!"

She couldn't see his face, but from the way he tensed, she could guess he didn't look happy. Not that either of them was happy, dangling off the edge of the world like this. "Swept-aways come here from somewhere else and take things that don't belong to them," he mumbled. "My family doesn't have as much as yours does, and it's because of people like you, coming here and taking everything that should be there for us. There's only so many fish in the river."

"I lived in an orphanage until I was nine," said Nadya. "We don't have swept-aways where I come from, but we didn't have enough food, either. We all had chores every day, and sometimes the younger kids couldn't finish theirs and they didn't get to eat. We'd save our rolls and sneak them to the little ones, but it wasn't easy. Nothing is *easy*. We don't take all the fish out of the river, either. There'd be plenty for you, if you could be nice long enough to convince a turtle to take you to the surface."

The boy didn't answer. Nadya scoffed. Much of the economy was based around fish, one way or another, and the only way to be a successful fisher was to convince a turtle to help you. If this boy had never put in the time, it was no wonder he was angry with her.

"Have you even tried for a turtle?"

"They said no, because I'm Belyyreka-born and my father has one," he blurted. "But Dmitri is old and he swims slow, and we never catch enough!"

Nadya frowned. That did seem unfair, but it wasn't her fault, and it wasn't as if she'd done it. Her arm was beginning to ache. She reached up with her right hand and grabbed the edge of the dock, pulling herself up, and the boy up with her.

Once they were both safely on the wood he stared at her, eyes wide as saucers. Nadya frowned.

"What?"

"Your *arm!*"

For the first time, it occurred to her that it was odd she'd been able to pull herself up with an arm she didn't have. She turned slowly and looked down at herself, then raised the right hand she wasn't meant to have and turned it back and forth in front of her face wonderingly.

The right arm she had never had was there now, a perfect mirror of her left, made of the dense, liquid kind of river water. It gleamed like quicksilver in the light. She raised her left hand and poked her right palm. Her finger slid easily through the skin, and she felt it, both the water on her finger and the tickling sensation of having something inside of her. Gasping, she jerked her hand away and scrambled to her feet, shaking her right arm like she thought she could shake it right off of her body.

"What is it what is it what is it?" she demanded. "Get it off!"

"It's the river!" The boy stood, still staring. "The River Wild chose you. I've never heard of a river-chosen swept-away before."

Nadya stopped shaking her hand and glared at him. "Keep talking riddles and I'll push you off the edge again."

"The river's magic. You have to know that by now."

Nadya nodded slowly. "I do."

"Well, sometimes, the river will choose someone to carry some of that magic with them, for their protection or because they'll benefit the river in some way. It chose you."

"Oh." Nadya looked at her new hand, turning it slowly back and forth. It didn't offend her the way the arm Pansy had forced upon her, all that time before, had; the river hadn't even offered it until she'd really needed a way to pull herself up to avoid being hurt. It wasn't because she wasn't good enough. It wasn't a way to make her look more normal. It was different and brilliant and special enough that the boy was looking at her with envy in his eyes, although that could also have been hunger.

"I said I would take a gift from a river, when I first got here," she said, slowly. "I said it where the river could hear me. So this is something I asked for, not something being forced on me. It doesn't change who I am. I'm allowed to want things to make the world a little easier. So thank you, river. It's beautiful."

Through her arm, she saw the shape of the harbormaster running along the dock toward them, with Burian in his wake. She made up her mind right there. Looking at the boy, she said firmly, "I need to know your name."

"Why?"

"Because Inna always wants me to get people's names before I bring them to the house. She says it's polite, and we have to be polite or people will think we're frogs washed over from the Winsome."

The boy shuddered. "Yuck, frogs."

"I saw one once."

"Really?"

"Really. It was when I first got here, before I even knew what Belyyreka meant, and—"

By the time the harbormaster reached them, they were chattering away and laughing like old friends. He stopped and stared, as much at Nadya's hand as at the sight of the two of them so chummy after what Burian had told him of the situation. Burian went to swim around his person, still anxious, and Nadya scratched the back of his head where she knew he liked it best with her new hand.

"Burian, this is Alexi, and he's very sorry he knocked me off the dock. He'll be coming to lunch with us today."

"But—" began Burian.

"No buts. He's hungry, and he's coming to lunch."

Burian grumbled something about stupid, soft-hearted humans and swam away, heading for the house. Nadya gave the harbormaster her best, most practiced smile. They had become close friends after her night in his house, and he checked on her often to be sure she was doing well with her new family.

"The arm is new," he observed, sounding half-amazed and half-amused.

"The river gave it to me when I was going to fall off the dock," said Nadya, holding up her right hand and turning it back and forth so he could see how perfect it was. "Do you think it's going to stay?"

"Gifts from the river generally do," said the harbormaster. "It's been a while since I've seen one, but I wouldn't worry about losing it."

Nadya, who wasn't worried, only curious, dimpled at him. "May we go?" she asked. "Alexi is hungry, and Burian is probably telling Inna some wild story by now."

"You may go," Ivan agreed, and watched as the children whirled and raced away, laughing between themselves.

Sometimes, he missed the resiliency of childhood more than words could say. But time was passing, and she wouldn't be that resilient forever. He just had to hope that every time she fell, the river would be there to catch her.

10 WHERE THE RIVER RUNS

TIME CONTINUED ON ITS WAY and in its way, passing for everyone at the same speed, swift and unstoppable as the River Wild itself. Alexi became a common sight in Inna's kitchen; they might not be able to feed every hungry child in the city, or force every parent to become a better person than they were, but they could feed him, and that was better than nothing by such a measure as to be immeasurable. Nadya's arm of River-water remained, as flexible and dexterous as any other human arm, and she accordingly spent more time on the fishing boats, no longer needing sticks to help her tie her knots.

She learned to catch small fish inside her palm and let them swim through the substance of her arm through the days, before releasing them back into the river. She found a tadpole, once, of the sort of frog that never grew larger than a grown man's hand, and she kept it cradled in her arm as it grew, watching its slow metamorphosis until the day it pulled itself free and hopped away, needing her no longer. She learned.

She watched the way people reacted to her River-arm, the ones who saw it as a useful tool and the ones who saw it as some sort of repair to the substance of her self, and she cleaved closer to the former and let the latter drift away. There was nothing wrong with using useful tools, or with having only a single hand to your name. She was herself, either way. It was just that now she was the version of herself who carried a river's love close against her skin, who could be a home to fish and frogs.

And then came the morning when Burian came to her window, sticking his head inside before the rest of the house was awake. "Hey," he said. "Hey, Nadya, hey."

"What?" She rolled over in her hammock and sat up, wiping sleep from her eyes with both hands, a gesture that had developed so quickly and so naturally that anyone who hadn't known her before her fall would never have guessed that her water arm was a recent development. She used it as naturally as she used her arm of flesh, and rarely seemed to mark the difference at all.

"I've just been to see Anna."

Nadya sat up straighter. Anna saw to the health and care of all the turtles who chose to live within the city—and some of those who didn't, who would still come to seek her out when they were hurt or sick or gravid and egg-bound. Even wild things can need care, and when lucky, they can seek it. Due to the damage to Burian's shell, Anna had been leery of letting him leave the creche in the first place, and had monitored his growth ever since. "What did she say?"

"She says I'm strong enough to go to the surface," he said, and then added, voice dipping so that it was almost shy, "She says I'm strong enough to ride."

Nadya slid out of her hammock and rushed to the window, putting her hands on the edge and leaning out so that she and Burian were face-to-face. "Truly?"

"Truly. They'll fit me for a saddle this afternoon, if you want them to."

Nadya squealed and boosted herself out the window so she could wrap her arms around her friend's neck and squeeze him to her. She would never have been able to embrace a

normal turtle that way, but Burian was intelligent; he could speak, he could tell her if she was hurting him, and he quite enjoyed the attention.

When she let go, he ducked his head and said, "I'm sorry it's taken so long. I'm sorry I can't pull a boat like Vasyl can. I'm sorry—"

"Don't be sorry about any of those things," she said, cutting him off. "Who wants to spend their life on a fishing boat? The river called me, and that means the river wants me to see more than just the common currents. Riders get to explore and find things we don't know about yet. You and I can go all the way to the Winsome if we want to, or to the Whimsy, or even to the Widdershins! We can see the whole world, and that's better than a boat. I'd rather you than the strongest turtle in the whole world."

"Really?"

"Really-really. You and me, Burian, we're going to swim all the way to the sky."

They went to Anna that afternoon to get Burian fitted with his saddle, which was braided rope and leather and stretched across his shell, tied at his belly. Only turtles who truly trusted their human companions to have their safety in mind agreed to be ridden; once the saddle was secured, the turtle couldn't remove it on their own. It would have to be refitted as he grew, and he still had quite a bit of growing to do; river turtles could be so large that even the tallest man in the world couldn't touch both sides of their shell at once, although it took them many, many years to reach that point. Burian would be small enough to be quick and agile for decades yet.

Most of the truly epic turtles swam away from the city, vanishing into the distant depths of Belyyreka, where their smaller relations couldn't go. They lived so long that they saw the companions of their youth age and die while they went ever on, as enduring as the river. It ate at them, to be left so alone, and isolation seemed to be the best response.

Nadya found it all very sad. More than once, she had hugged Burian by the neck and whispered, "I won't ever go away. I won't ever leave you. We'll find a way for me to live with you forever, and even when you get as big as a boat, I'll still be bringing you biscuits and scolding you for sneaking up on me."

"Lots of turtles get as big as boats," said Burian.

"Big as an *island*, then! Big as a whole *house*!" She wasn't actually sure which of those two things was bigger, but it seemed to be the right thing to say, every time she said it. Here and now, standing back and watching as Burian was fitted, she half-listened to the lecture Anna was delivering on the responsibility attendant with being a turtle-rider, how important it was that she never go anywhere without telling Inna and the harbormaster where they were going to be and when they were going to be back. Things could happen to riders. Bad things, even, when no one knew how to find and help them.

Nadya bristled at the implication that she and Burian wouldn't be able to handle anything that came their way. She was brave and clever and almost grown! She had been in Belyyreka for so long that no traces of the world she'd come from remained, her clothes long since gone to rot and dissolution, her shoes replaced a dozen times, even her body changed by the passing of time and the pressures of puberty. She might not be an adult yet, even as the river measured such things, but she was closer than she was distant, and she could handle herself and her companion when she needed to. But she smiled and thanked Anna for the advice all the same, and Anna, who had seen hundreds of hopeful riders come through, reins in their hands and dreams of adventure in their eyes, knew full well that not all of them came back.

And some of those who did didn't come back complete. They lost their steeds or they lost pieces of themselves, and the river didn't always see fit to gift them with replacements as it had Nadya. She could lose more than she imagined if she wasn't careful, and Anna wanted to spare her and Burian both the pain of that, if she could.

But she couldn't, of course, and she knew that even as she lectured and Nadya's eyes shone with the thrill of her impending freedom. No one can warn the eager and excited away from their own future. A future is a monster of its own breed, different for everyone, and ever inescapable.

Nadya and Burian left the city together the minute they were cleared, not even stopping by the house to get sandwiches from Inna.

They had a world to see.

NADYA HELD HER BREATH as they broke the surface of the River Wild, an old reflex that always seemed to take over when she approached a transition between the types of water. Burian gasped, taking a breath of the thinner water above, and looked down at the river's surface, which seemed suddenly so much thicker than it had been from below.

"Nadya, your arm?" he asked, turning his head to look at her.

She smiled and held up her right hand, wiggling her fingers at him. "It always stays. The river gave it to me, and it's mine now." She had been worried, the first time she rode the boats up into the above-river to fish, that it would stay below. It was an easy thing, to grow accustomed to having an arm, even after spending so much time without one. She would do fine without it, but if she could keep it, that was her preference. Like a knife or a fisher's hook, it was an easy tool that made things easier.

"Ah," said Burian, who never accompanied the fishing boat. That was Vasyl's territory. He looked around, to the endless river in one direction and the towering wood in the other. "Where shall we go?"

The fishing boats rarely went ashore. The farming boats did, to plant and tend and harvest, but Inna's house was a fishing house, and so Nadya had rarely been entirely outside the River Wild since coming to Belyyreka. "The wood," she said. "The flooded forest. I had . . . I had a friend there once. I wonder if he might still be around."

She didn't know how long foxes lived, but with everything else in Belyyreka being the way it was, it might be a long, long time. Maybe they were like turtles and simply got larger as they aged, and when she approached the forest's edge, a fox the size of a horse would come trotting out to meet her. Burian nodded and turned against the current, swimming toward the shore.

He was no tortoise, to spend his days on dry land and walk everywhere, but neither was he a sea turtle, with wide paddles for legs and no real grace on land. As they reached the shallows, his swimming became walking, until finally he was standing and stepping up onto the shore, clawed feet digging into the mud. His belly skirted the ground, and Nadya shifted uncomfortably atop him, feeling the weight of the thin-water world settle on her shoulders. They weren't dry here—what she had taken for dryness on her first arrival was simply a different form of damp, delicate and so all-encompassing it was almost imperceptible—but she *felt* dry by comparison. She felt like she was edging back toward the world of her birth, and she never wanted to return there. Not today, not ever. She was sure.

Burian stopped near the edge of the wood, looking dubiously at the trees. "They seem very close together," he said. "I'm not sure I can go in there."

Nadya slid off his back. "It's all right," she said. "You don't have to go into the woods. If we want to see the River Winsome, we'll have to find a way around, but that can happen later, when everyone's more used to us coming and going." She gave his shell a pat, then took a few steps toward the tree line, pausing a decent distance back to cup her hands around her mouth and call, "Artyom! Artyom the fox!"

She waited until the echoes of her shout had faded before she turned back to Burian, trying not to look as disappointed as she felt. "I suppose it was silly to hope he'd still be here, it's been so long," she said. "I just thought this part of the wood might be his home."

"It was," said a voice behind her. She turned again, and there was a fox sitting at the edge of the wood, fur a rosy gold, tail wrapped around its feet. It was watching her with sharp, clever eyes, body tensed in a way that told her it would bolt and disappear if she took so much as a step in its direction. "He's not here anymore."

"Did he move elsewhere in the wood?"

"No." The fox continued to watch her with sharp, sharp eyes. "A frog came out of the River Winsome ages ago and ate him up with a snap. He was my grandfather."

It didn't ease the sting to know that while time might be different for foxes, her friend the fox had died by other means. Nadya grimaced. "I'm so sorry."

"Did you know him?"

"He helped me cross the flooded forest when I was just a little girl."

The fox looked at her. "You're the human child he found on the banks of the Winsome. Nadezhda."

No one called Nadya by the full form of her name anymore, but it made something in her chest feel warm to know that Artyom had remembered her. She had never forgotten him, exactly, but somehow time had gotten away from her down beneath the river, and she'd been able to convince herself, time and again, that one day soon she would go to the surface with the intent to go back into the flooded forest, one day soon she would let him know she was all right. One day.

And somewhere in the middle of all those unkept promises, a terrible thing had come out of another river and swallowed him down, quick as anything. It wasn't fair. It was still true.

"My name is Artem," said the fox. "He spoke well of you, my grandfather did. Said you were quick and clever and willing to listen when he told you what to do. He rarely spoke that well of humans."

"I was very lost and he helped me find my home," said Nadya, voice small. "I was grateful. I still am."

"Then go home," said Artem. "Get back on your turtle and go back beneath the surface of the river and be happy, human child. Never come here again. The flooded forest is not for you."

Nadya blinked. Of all the welcomes she could have expected, this was the least expected. "I'm a rider now," she said. "We scout for the city, to find good fishing and good farmland. It's my duty to be here."

"Do you really think there's anything left along the river's length that your people haven't already seen and studied and learned to understand?" asked Artem. "Humans are curious things. They want to *know*. They want the answers to questions that had no business ever being asked, and so they're never truly sure of anything, not even their own desires. They're too busy chasing their tails to see the rabbits. There are no wonders for you here, Nadezhda. No mysteries to solve, no monsters to fight. Only a place you need not be, like so many other places you need not be. Only a danger."

Nadya blinked at him, then blinked again as Burian's great head pushed its way under her right hand, lifting it up.

"The river chose her, fox," he said. "The world chose her and then the river chose her, and she'll go where she wishes to go, and I'll go with her, as I am her companion and you are not."

Artem slitted his eyes in what could have been amusement and could have been annoyance, regarding Burian for a long, silent moment before he leapt to his feet and went bounding off, stopping at the edge of both the wood and Nadya's hearing to look back at her and say ominously, "Go back below, where you've already drowned, and leave the dry world to its own devices."

Then he was gone, darting off into the trees. Burian walked ponderously forward, nudging the brush at the edge of the wood with his nose.

"What are you doing?" Nadya asked.

"We have to cross the wood somehow," said Burian.

"I thought you didn't think you'd fit between the trees."

"I didn't. I still don't, but if that fox wants to tell you that we can't be here, we're going to be here all the more." Burian twisted his neck, looking back at her. "The river chose you. *I* chose you. No one else gets to tell you where you're meant to be."

Nadya frowned, not quite sure of the logic, but she allowed Burian to lead her along the forest's edge until the sky started to darken with a coming storm. Then she coaxed him back to the river, and they returned to the depths, following the fleet of fishing boats that also raced ahead of the rain. Perhaps the forest would be easier to travel when it was actually flooded, and not simply haunted by the ghosts of past rainfall.

Burian grumbled during the first part of their descent, but by the time they leveled out into their final approach to the city, he was happy again, proud of the journey they had taken together. He came to a stop in front of Inna's house, and Nadya slid down from his back onto the dock. "Do you want me to remove the saddle?" she asked.

"Anna will do it," he replied, nudging her with his head. "She prefers to remove the saddles herself, to be sure there's no tangle in the cords or breakage in the knots."

"I'll have to learn to do it eventually."

"Not today. Today is for celebrating what we've done." Burian bumped her with his head again. "I'll have my saddle off and be given the finest greens and fish, and it will be a beautiful night. Your family will be ready to feast with you. I know Inna will have asked Alexi to join you, and if you're not there, he won't be able to enjoy the splendor of a welcome feast. So go. Go, and tomorrow, we'll go up to the surface again. We'll find our way through that wood, and we'll see the Winsome."

"All right," said Nadya, and kissed the top of his head before turning and going into the house, which was low and bright and filled with laughter. Inna met her in the front room, grabbing her by the waist and spinning her around before leading her to the table, where Galina and her husband and their children were waiting. Places had been set for

Nadya and another for Alexi. She looked at the empty chair and blinked.

"Inna?"

"He's coming," said Inna warmly. "He'll be here soon, I'm sure of that if nothing else."

"I'm glad," said Nadya.

"How did you enjoy the surface?"

Nadya hesitated before saying, "It was very . . . dry. I know everything of Belyyreka is under the great lake, and the water extends above the river's surface, but it felt so much like the air from the world where we were born. It was thin and dry and I didn't like it."

"The different forms of water can seem very strange when you move between them," said Inna kindly. "If you touch your arm, does it feel wet?"

"Yes," said Nadya hesitantly, and pressed her fingers against the surface of her right arm, letting them dip just below the surface. And it did feel wet, in a way the world around her didn't. She pulled her hand back. "I know we're under the river, and everything around us is water, but my arm still feels like water. It's wet, like the world isn't."

"The water of your arm is from the bottom of the river," said Galina's husband, a broad, amiable man who worked the farms downriver during the days, gathering greens and fresh fruit for the city below. His boat went up with the fishermen, and came down at the same time, delivering their wares to market along with the fish and crabs. Many things would grow above the river but not below.

"The water there is heavier," said Nadya hesitantly. "That's why it sinks to the bottom."

"The water above the river is lighter, which is why it stays there," said Galina's husband. "And the lighter water becomes, the drier it seems against the skin."

Nadya frowned. "We went to the edge of the forest where you found me, Inna. The fox who led me through wasn't there. He died. But his grandson was there, and he told us to stay away, that the forest wasn't for humans. Can he do that? Can a fox tell us to stay out of a whole forest?"

"Of course he can," said Inna. "He did, didn't he? Whether he has any authority to make saying it mean anything more than sounds is another question."

"Well, does he?"

"Foxes do not control the forests, but there are other things than foxes in the trees. Burian is a fine, strong young turtle, but he would be unable to defend you from a bear, if one took a liking to the smell of you, or a wolf, if it hungered."

Nadya swallowed. She was about to ask how many wolves and bears there were in the forest, and whether it was really a good idea for her and Burian to go scouting alone—not that she wanted to give up her newfound freedom, but she was even less eager to be eaten by a bear—when Alexi came rushing in.

"I was at the market," he said. He had been working one of the stalls there for the past year, selling vegetables during shopping times, sweeping and helping with the inventory when crowds were thin. He might, if he liked, take an apprenticeship with one of the farming boats in the next year, to begin heading above-river to the fields. They had discussed it, in the halting, awkward way teens talked about the future when they didn't want to face it directly, out of fear that it would come swooping down and gobble them up; he had no interest in fishing and, with no turtle of his own, couldn't be a scout. He did well enough at the market, and might choose to be a merchant instead of a farmer.

It would be better than following in the footsteps of his parents, who were scavengers and thieves, and had never sought a job in service of the city. Not everyone could work; some were too sick or too old or, as they had been until recently, too young. And they were cared for as much as possible. In Alexi's case, the assumption had been that his parents would provide for him, and when they had failed to do so, his stomach had gone empty and his resentments had grown wild.

A few hot meals and the care of a family, even if it wasn't entirely his own, had done a great deal to prune those resentments away. He rushed to settle next to Nadya, asking, "Am I late?"

"No, we haven't started yet," said Inna reassuringly. She smiled at the two of them. Alexi might not be family now, but she felt sure he would be in the not-too-distant future. He and Nadya were growing up so quickly, settling into their places within the city, the roles they were going to play in their adult lives. She couldn't imagine they weren't going to spend those lives together. Nadya had plenty of friends, scuffling, roiling urchins who spilled in and out of the house like hatchling turtles, but none of them had become family the way Alexi was beginning to.

None of them had near-permanent places at the table or watched Nadya with the same burgeoning awe. And so Inna kept smiling at Alexi as she placed rolls on his plate and waved for Galina's daughter to pass the tray of roast rabbit down the table. Each of the people at the table served and was served in turn, until their plates were piled high with delicacies, and Inna clapped her hands for their attention.

"We have come together over this bread and this bone to celebrate the passage of one of our own into the halls of adulthood," she said. "Our Nadya and her Burian have become scouts on this day, traveling to the lands above the river to enhance the glory of our city!"

Cheers erupted around the table. Nadya's cheeks reddened as she ducked her head in pleased embarrassment, staring at her plate like it might hold the secrets of her life as yet to come.

"Nadya is the first scout of our household, and so we applaud her bravery and quickness, to go where so few have gone before her, into the waters and the wilds. She will bring much honor to our house, until she leaves us to open a house of her own." More applause.

Nadya's cheeks grew redder. It was understood that although she was the oldest of the three children of the house, she was also the most recently arrived; she wouldn't be the one to inherit, but would one day be the one to strike out and open a house of her own. This house belonged to Inna, who had been adopted before Galina arrived to her parents, and Galina's husband had come along still later. Galina's son would be the owner of the household one day, and while he would never turn Nadya out, he would most likely take a spouse of his own, or his sister would, and they would fill all the available space. It was thus expected that Nadya would be the one to find another place.

It was a fair and reasonable means of doing things. Nadya still didn't like to think about it more than she had to. She no longer knew how old she was, not really; she knew she had been almost eleven when she'd fallen into the pond, and that based on her height and . . . other factors . . . she was probably somewhere around nineteen by now, but she couldn't say exactly. There were no seasons in the River Wild, aside from "storm" and "not storm," and sometimes they were long seasons and sometimes they were short seasons, and no one really knew how to predict which was going to be which. Time seemed to matter less, at the bottom of the river.

"Bears," said Nadya, looking to Inna. "You mentioned bears. How concerned do I need to be about bears?"

None of the conversations she had had about scouting had mentioned bears, or wolves. They hadn't dwelt on the flooded forest, either, but on the farmlands and what might be beyond them, distant and drowning. The expectation had always seemed to be that she would strike out downriver or upriver, not take Burian and go overland.

Had she been river-born, or landed first in the Wild and not the Winsome, that might have been a reasonable expectation. Children who were born to the Wild seemed to think "Wild" was another word for "world," and that anything beyond the river's banks was not meant for them to know. Only the swept-away scouts went any farther, and she hadn't heard of anyone going to the Winsome in years.

"The bears are only in the forests," said Alexi. "The elders teach us about them when we ask about farming, because sometimes they'll come out of the wood to try and steal what we're growing. Ivan was a baker before he became harbormaster, and he says they used to set the burnt loaves out for the bears to come and take, because if they shared, the bears didn't raid them and knock over their ovens. The bears are as smart as the foxes, and they can be reasoned with, if there's no other choice."

"Still, bears," said Galina, and shivered exaggeratedly. "You'll never find me scouting or farming or baking or hunting or anything else that means being above-river and off the boats long enough to have to deal with them!"

"Wolves are smarter," said Galina's husband, in his ponderous way. "They make plans and carry grudges, sometimes for generations. Best never to truck with wolves."

Nadya made a noncommittal sound and poked her dinner with her fork, suddenly feeling less like she was celebrating than being condemned. None of the lectures she'd received about the dangers of scouting had mentioned wolves or bears. She and Burian might have set their hearts on something else if they'd known, baking or hunting or another profession that was easier with personal transport but didn't require her companion to tow a boat as he swam. It seemed like a cheat, somehow, to allow her to commit herself to filling a role for the city that carried dangers she didn't fully understand along with it.

It felt like the sort of unkindness that had driven Alexi to challenge and fight her on the dock, people not sharing things that other people needed to know, and it tarnished her joy, making it hard to enjoy a meal that contained so many of her favorite things, or the company of so many of her favorite people.

After dinner was done and the dishes cleared, Nadya and Alexis walked along the docks hand in hand, her watery fingers tangled through his fleshy ones. "It's like they don't *want* us to know what's above before we get there and it's too late for us to say no," she complained.

"There used to be another city, in the Winsome," he said. "My father used to talk about it, when he'd been drinking and wanted something to be angry about that wasn't me or my mother."

Nadya focused on him. "Oh?"

"He lived there when he was a boy. I think half the stories he tells about it are remembering something he can't have anymore as better than anything he could possibly have now to make himself feel better about how badly he's done since the city fell. But he said it was as big and beautiful as our own, and the people who lived there didn't have turtles."

"So how did they get anything done?"

"They had river otters instead, big as boats, who pulled them up and down as was needed. And they harvested oysters more than fish. The Winsome feeds into a vast estuary of salted water."

"An ocean?" asked Nadya, wonderingly. She had never heard of an ocean in Belyyreka before.

"That's not the word he used, but I suppose, if it's something you know." Alexi sighed. "Frogs overran them. They swallowed up the children and the smallest of the otters, and the otters who remained abandoned them, and so they were forced to flee the river and travel overland until they reached the River Wild. It's why he never let me go to take care of the hatchlings when I was young enough that one of them might have decided to choose me for their companion. He said companions can't be trusted, because they'll always leave you when you need them the most."

"That's just silly," said Nadya. "Otters and turtles aren't the same, and even if they were, running away when something is eating your babies isn't abandoning, it's being smart." She knew enough to know that Galina would never leave her children, but if something ate them, she would probably leave everything that remained behind rather than stay where they had been but weren't any longer.

"I guess." They walked a little farther in silence, before

Alexi said, "I'm talking to Kristof about taking a seat on one of the farming boats with the next growing season. I like plants. I think I could do well in the fields."

"Then it sounds like a good thing for you."

"I know it's not very exciting, farming, but it's good work, and it fills tables."

"Tables, and market stalls." Galina's husband brought home produce to feed the family, sometimes more than they could eat, and still had enough to sell and bring back a reasonable amount of coin. The city didn't depend on money as much as it did on barter, but sometimes money was needed for the things that didn't keep long enough to be reliably traded. The water in the river was breathable, but it made it difficult to keep baked goods or meat for long before they would grow a thick coat of mildew and become something that wasn't any good for eating. And money was less awkward than charging dried fish to charge for painting a house or potatoes for a trip to the doctor.

It was a day-by-day economy, sustained by the environment's passive interference with any form of hoarding or resource complication, and Nadya loved it. No one was wealthy. No one who had the ability to work and chose to actually do so was poor. They all had enough.

"Tables and market stalls," Alexi agreed. "I'm decent enough at it, and I could be good if I do it for a while. Good enough to grow fruit and herbs and other nice things for a table to have."

Nadya had been in Belyyreka long enough to recognize the shape of this conversation. She bit her lip in thought as they continued on. The docks had long since become familiar territory to her. Most of the city had, and the ebb and flow of its days was something she understood down to the bottom of her bones. One day, those bones would be a part of the city's foundations, and she would rest easily. But until then, there were things to do, choices to be made, a life to be led.

"I won't be able to stay at home and raise children as Galina has done," she said. "I'm far too fond of Burian and I like scouting. It's what I want to do."

"I've always liked staying home," said Alexi. "It's very possible to farm and also do the majority of the work of raising children."

Nadya, who had done her share of childrearing at the orphanage and had not discovered an urge to do more of the same in her time under the river, made a noncommittal noise.

"It's also possible to have a home with no children," said Alexi. "My father's line comes from a fallen city, my mother's has been carried on by two sisters. If I choose not to have children of my own, but to call a swept-away or two my sons and daughters, it will cost the river nothing, and I can still be happy with my contributions."

"Scouting carries dangers," warned Nadya. "There might be a day when I don't come back."

"Boats sink when storms come in too quickly for the turtles to take them below the surface, and if the transition isn't made smoothly, people can drown," said Alexi. "Frogs come out of the forest and attack the farmers. I would be expected to do my share of standing guard, if I went to the fields. There might be a day when I don't come back, either."

Nadya looked deep into her heart and found no further objections. She stopped walking, still holding Alexi's hand, and turned to face him.

"I think I would like to have a home with you," she said.

He smiled, bright as anything. "Really?" He pulled his hand from hers and used it to move the hair away from her face.

"Really," she replied, and kissed him.

11 A LIFETIME

TIME DID NOT START MOVING faster after that, although it felt as if it did. Alexi went to the farms and Nadya scouted every day with Burian, exploring the land above the river. Most scouts chose to stay on the Wild, observing what could be seen from the water, taking note of clear land that might be of interest to the farmers or of good fishing grounds or hunting territory. They thought Nadya and Burian wild and brave for venturing onto the land.

Nadya honestly wasn't sure why they bothered going up if they were never going to leave the Wild. Every inch of the river had been covered before, and everything they saw had been seen a dozen times before, sometimes in the same season. Things would change after a large storm, the banks shifting, the fish changing their spawning grounds, but storms large enough to reshape the river were rare. But they all got paid the same for their time, coins enough to squirrel away, to begin saving toward the rapidly approaching future. It was worth it. It was enough.

Nadya herself continued her explorations into the edges of the flooded forest, which was always damp and swampy but had yet to actually flood in her presence. She saw Artem the fox several more times, and each time he warned her away, while Burian explored the edges of the wood, looking for a way in large enough to accommodate his girth. She found more of the berry bushes she remembered from her trip through the forest, and returned to that area the next day with a bucket, filling it to the brim and bringing it proudly home to Inna, who baked sweet hand pies and gave her half as her reward for gathering.

Time passed. The wedding, when it came, was small and simple, as befit a poor man from the lower part of the city and a swept-away who was last child of her house but first to be wed. The harbormaster officiated the ceremony, which was held outside behind the creche with Burian and all the unattached turtles in attendance, swirling around the guests in great, giddy spirals. By the end of the day, when the last of the jam tarts had been eaten and the wedding plates had been ceremonially smashed, the younger of Galina's children had a small turtle attending her every move, and Nadya was smiling so hard her face hurt, not quite sure any longer how this could be her life.

She had been in Belyyreka for so long that she barely re-membered the neighborhood where she'd been living with Carl and Pansy, remembered none of the names of the chil-dren at the school she'd been attending, not even the ones she'd considered her friends, remembered few of the matrons from the orphanage. But she remembered Maksim, and she remembered ice cream, and if it was odd that those were the only two things she ever missed from her old life, there was no one to tell her so. Not even Alexi, who found her description of ice cream interesting but not alluring, and never mocked her for missing a tortoise she had left in another country even before she left it in another world.

When they walked together into the small but empty house that would be their home from now on, to fill with love and laughter and whatever else happened to come their way, both of them still in their wedding finery, all of it Inna's work—for both of them, as Alexi's mother didn't know how to embroider and had been happy to send her son to his own marriage in a plain shirt—and Nadya with flowers braided in her hair and floating in the substance of her liquid arm, they were hand in hand, as they so often were. Alexi let go, pulling shyly away, and Nadya went after him, and they came together into what would ever afterward be their bedroom. It wasn't the largest of the three rooms that could be used for that purpose, but they didn't need the largest; they needed the one with the best-placed window, for Burian's sake, and the most light, for the sake of Alexi's plants. Only a few would grow in the heavier water beneath the river, and all of them needed as much light as possible.

But for now, there were no plants, there was no turtle, there was nothing but Nadya and Alexi and the warm, flat surface of the bed, soft sand sewn into woven cloth to form a mattress, a blanket of water-treated rabbit fur atop it, and the two of them atop that, tangled in each other's arms and celebrating the beginning of a new life, a new tributary to swim. They would eat in their own home from now on, sleep in their own bed, and live in the city as adults, independent and contributing.

All that would begin tomorrow. Here and now, there were the two of them, and the room, and the discovery of each other's bodies, hands on skin and all the River Wild to see them as they truly were.

When they slept, it was tangled in each other's arms, peaceful and content and wholly sure of their place in their world.

The storm came rolling in the next day. It was the largest storm anyone had seen since before Nadya's arrival, strong enough to shake the city, even deep as it was below the surface, the rain pounding into the water and driving itself downward like falling knives. What fell from the sky began as heavy water—what Nadya couldn't help thinking of on some level as true water, the kind that could be drunk but not breathed—and it hurt to stand outside for too long.

All trips to the surface were canceled as people battened down and ate what they had in their homes, avoiding trips along the docks as much as possible. As for the docks themselves, they swayed alarmingly in the rough currents, and some segments broke off and dropped away, driven farther downward by the rain. Debris plummeting past the windows became a common sight, until the second day of the storm, when Nadya saw a body fall past and threw herself out the front door, shouting for Burian.

She flung herself over the edge of the dock, aiming for the body as it fell downward, still yelling in the vain hope that her beloved turtle would be close enough to hear her and intercede. She kicked to drive herself farther downward, swimming against water she could barely feel, and shot toward the body. It was a woman she didn't recognize, the embroidery around her cuffs and collar signaling that she was one of the farmers. Alexi might know her, but Alexi was still above, safely in their home, probably cursing the wildness of his wife.

"I hope this was worth the hiding I'll get when I get home," muttered Nadya. Unspoken was that she hoped she would *get* home. Falling was dangerous in part because the water was too thin to allow humans to swim back upward, and she had already fallen past at least five levels.

A trickle of blood ran down the woman's forehead, dark and thick. Something had hit her in the head, probably knocking her off the edge in the process. Nadya frowned as she swam closer, finally reaching out and grabbing the woman's arm. The woman's weight was too much for her to carry upward, and hard as she kicked, they continued to descend, until the water darkened around them and the lowest levels of the city flashed by, gray stone and white shell and then nothing apart from the stone outcropping this part of the city had been built atop. Nadya closed her eyes, expression going grim. She had never been this deep before.

She had always wanted to see the bottom of the river. She had never expected it to happen quite like this.

The woman was breathing. Nadya kicked harder, trying to slow their descent if nothing else. They would reach the bottom eventually, and she would rather delay that moment. Heavier water flowed downward, dropping through lighter water even as they were; all the rain and all the other heavy water that had entered the river would be at the very bottom. If they fell that far, they would drown. She had to at least try.

They didn't move any higher, didn't regain any of the ground they'd lost, didn't even stop falling, but it felt like they slowed down, and so she kept kicking. It might not be doing any actual good. It was better than doing nothing.

The wall of stone that held up the city was getting closer to them. It was clearly more of an underwater mountain than a sheer cliff. Nadya began kicking toward it, holding the woman against her, trying to reach something she could hang on to. A fish flashed by, one of the largest she had ever seen, moving with the ease she normally saw only near the surface, and it was getting harder to breathe. The water was definitely heavier here.

The idea of drowning in the river where she lived was ridiculous to her. It was stupid, it was impossible, and it was going to happen if she didn't move very quickly and get very lucky. She kicked again, harder than before, reaching out with her right hand to grab the wall.

Balls of rain were falling all around them, too heavy to join with the river. A string of them flowed into her hand, coalescing into a long rope with a loop at one end. Nadya took in a sharp breath, coughing as the increasing heaviness of the water stung her lungs and the back of her throat, and hurled the loop as hard as she could at the wall.

She had never lassoed anything in her life. She didn't even know the name for the tool she was attempting to use. There was no grace or elegance to the move, no sign that she had any idea what she was doing, and so no one could have been more surprised than she when the "rope" snagged around an outcropping of rock. She tightened her hold on the woman and stopped kicking as they fell, allowing the rope to snap taut and swing them up against the wall.

Impact wasn't as hard as it would have been if they'd been falling in the air of the world where Nadya had been born, but was hard enough to be jarring and make Nadya's teeth rattle. She managed not to lose her grip on the woman, and she *couldn't* lose her grip on the rope, which was connected to her hand in a way that made it more like a finger than an actual tool.

Holding that comparison firmly in mind, she began pulling herself up the rope, pausing every few seconds to think about how nice and convenient it would be if the rope were shorter, if she didn't have to worry about dropping back to the place where they first stopped. Her shoulders ached, her torso felt tight and too small, the effort of the climb reverberated through every inch of her body, and still she climbed, even as the woman she held so tightly against her began to whimper and stir.

When the woman opened her eyes, she screamed.

Nadya winced. "Stop that. You're right against my ear."

"Y-you're Inna's girl," said the woman, still terrified. "The scout."

"Yes, and right now we're both very far from the city, although straight down isn't usually a direction I scout in!" Nadya continued pulling them along. The rope wasn't pooling in her hand or dangling beneath them; it did indeed seem to be getting shorter at her silent command. That was something. "Can you hold on to me if I let go?"

The woman shrieked and thrashed. "Don't let go, don't let go!"

"I'm not going to let you fall, but this would go faster if I could pull us up with both hands," snapped Nadya. "Can you hold on?"

The woman hesitated, then snaked her arms around Nadya's neck, clinging so tight that for a moment, Nadya couldn't breathe. Then the woman slackened her grip and Nadya exhaled, relieved, before saying, "Good," unwinding her own arm from around the woman, and beginning to pull them upward with both hands.

It *was* faster this way, and in short order they had reached the outcropping where her rope was snagged, and she was able to pull them onto the narrow ledge. They fell no farther. She looked up. The wall was sheer and impassable. Nadya sighed, watching as the rope melted back into her arm. "We may be here awhile," she said. "I suppose you'd best tell me your name."

12 BACK THROUGH THE FLOODED FOREST

NADYA AND THE WOMAN (whose name was Anichka; she was a farmer, and had been bringing in the herbs and simples from her garden when the storm swept her off the dock and began her fall) sat and talked for what felt like hours before there were lights above them, and voices shouting Nadya's name. She leapt to her feet, waving her arms in the air.

"Here! We're here!" she called.

Several great turtles descended, all larger than her beloved Burian, all equipped to swim these depths without losing control. Ivan the harbormaster sat astride the largest of them, a harpoon in one hand and a lantern in the other. Inna was on another, the first time Nadya had seen the woman who had become in all ways her mother astride a turtle. She blinked. Inna pressed a hand to her breast, staring at Nadya like she had never seen anything so wonderful. Nadya offered her a smile in return.

Anichka shrank back against the stone wall, suddenly shy, as Nadya stood and pulled her to her feet. "Have you come to get us?" Nadya asked, intentionally insouciant.

Ivan smiled. "No. We just wanted to see how far you'd fallen, and now we'll leave you here. Of course we've come to get you, foolish girl. We would have come faster, but the we had to allow the storm time to pass."

"Alexi is very concerned," scolded Inna. "Most men don't care to see their wives go flinging themselves over the edge of the world. Come, we'll have you back to him, and calmed, before we waste a moment more."

"Come, Anichka," said Nadya. She leapt from the ledge, catching the rope Ivan threw down to hold her, and let herself be pulled onto the back of his turtle, where he embraced her and looked her over for injuries, as Inna tossed a matching rope to Anichka. The turtles grumbled at the added weight, but as two passengers were less than the balance of a boat, they bore up well enough, and began swimming back toward the city, cutting smoothly through the weighted water.

The devastation of the storm became more and more apparent as they drew nearer home. Docks had been smashed, markets washed away, houses stove in by the weight of debris falling on them from above or whirled up by the currents raging below. Nadya stopped looking after she saw a young turtle crushed under a wall, motionless. They would be rebuilding from this for years, if not forever.

No, it couldn't be forever. As they reached the level where she and Alexi lived, and she saw him standing outside their house, twisting a rag between his large, well-loved hands, a worried expression on his face, she knew it couldn't be forever. There had been storms before. There would be storms again. They would rebuild, ever and always.

Ivan kissed her forehead and pushed her toward her husband, and she paddled across the short distance between them, arms and legs churning to keep herself from falling through the thin water, which was never meant to hold a human up for very long. His eyes lit up, and then his whole face with them, and he dropped the rag as he opened his arms and welcomed her home again.

They broke their kiss when Inna's turtle brought her to a level with their faces. "You will go and apologize to Burian for frightening him so," she said. "And you will come to dinner with us tonight, to talk about why you are a foolish girl who shouldn't risk yourself for others when there's any other choice."

"But there wasn't, Inna," said Nadya. "Anichka was falling, and there was no one else to jump."

"That may be so, and she seems a lovely lady, but you are my daughter, and my concern is for you before any other."

"Thank you, Inna."

"Be safer, Nadya." Inna sighed and turned her turtle upward, taking Anichka with her, and the others of the rescue party swam away one by one, leaving Nadya alone with Alexi.

She looked at him, suddenly shy. "Are you very angry with me?"

"Angry? No. I knew who I was marrying when I made the choice to offer for you. A little sad, perhaps, but glad of the time we'll have together, and that they brought you home to me."

"I'll always come home to you," promised Nadya, as he let her go.

"I know," he said, and smiled as he watched her run off along the dock toward the building where the turtles were housed.

The trip took twice the time it should have, as she dodged around holes in the dock and paused to help people clear debris from doorways and, yes, bodies. But the path was familiar, for all the damage that had been done, and in fairly short order she was running through the door, waving to a wide-eyed Anna, and heading into the large room where the adult turtles sheltered during storms and the like.

Burian met her almost as soon as she stepped inside. "They

wouldn't let me go with the others to bring you home!" he wailed.

"Why not?"

"There are fish down deep, big fish with big jaws, and a bite from one them could have split my shell in two and they didn't think it would help if they found you but lost me!"

"Oh, Burian." Nadya tried not to think of the shadows she'd seen moving below them, or how close they might have come to dropping into the domain of those very fish. No point in dwelling on it now. "You are the bravest, smartest turtle I know, and I'm so glad you didn't risk yourself for me. Now come on."

"Where are we going?"

She smiled, impish and wicked. "The storm will have raised the level of the river. The forest may well be flooded again. Come, we'll get you saddled."

THEY RODE TOGETHER to the top of the river, the girl with the arm of River-water clinging to the back of the great turtle with the scarred shell, and when their heads broke the surface, they looked out together on a world transformed.

The river had indeed risen, and it was good that at least one of the scouts had gone up to see it for herself; when they went back down, Nadya would have to tell Alexi to notify the other farmers that their fields were well and truly swamped. In rising, the river had also spread, reaching watery hands across the landscape to grasp at everything it could reach. The trees of the forest resembled the rickety pickets of a fence, some of them leaning at odd angles, others fallen entirely, and the water spread between those same trees, flowing outward, carrying the flood in its open arms.

Burian swam forward, Nadya clinging to his back, and exclaimed in wordless delight when he found that between the fallen trees and the water, he could fit easily into the wood, traveling faster and farther than he had ever been before. Nadya laughed, looking around her at this swamped and flooded world as they traveled through. Here at the surface, the water of the river—the water of the flood—looked like any pond or river in the world of her birth, heavy and smooth.

It was water as she knew it instinctively, water you could drown in, and she was glad to have Burian beneath her as they traveled through the forest, where she knew the ground to be an endless succession of snarled roots and rocks, to catch her feet and trip her. She could have fallen and drowned in the wood, had she attempted the crossing on her own.

Artem the fox appeared atop a fallen tree, watching them silently as they passed. She looked forward, trying to see the forest's edge. When she glanced back, he was gone.

She frowned and returned her attention to the journey. Burian had never been here before. He needed her guidance.

Not that there was much to guide. She had traveled straight through the forest on her first visit, and so Burian did the same, or as close to the same as his size and the pattern of the fallen trees would allow. The water shallowed out for a while, and when it began to deepen again, she knew that they had crossed the line between the two rivers; they were approaching the Winsome.

Nadya sat up straighter, unmistakable excitement surging through her. They had done it. They had crossed the uncrossable forest, and she was going to see the river the humans had been forced to surrender after the other Belyyrekan city had fallen. She leaned forward, patting Burian on the neck.

"Look," she cried, jubilant. "We're almost there! We can go home with oysters and information, and everyone will applaud us!"

"I hope oysters are worth all this distance," grumbled Burian, but she could tell he was as pleased as she was, and when they emerged from the trees into the water at the river's edge, she fancied she could feel his excitement flowing up through her hands where they clutched the rim of his shell. They had become scouts because they enjoyed the process of learning their world, and this was something entirely new to learn.

The River Winsome was as she remembered it, only more so, fat and swollen with rain, so full it looked like a bubble on the verge of bursting. Where its waters brushed up against those of the River Wicked, which ran in the opposite direction, a thick band of white, churning foam formed, the two rivers warring for ownership of the current. Nadya wasn't sure whether there would be a winner, but she was quite sure that anyone foolish enough to go near that roiling line would regret it.

Burian paddled forward, until they were well clear of the trees and unquestionably in the Winsome itself. "Which way?" he asked.

Nadya considered. "Downriver," she said finally. "Alexi said it ends in an estuary, and estuaries normally mean oceans. I'd like to know if that's the case here, too."

"What's an ocean?" asked Burian.

"And that's the other reason I'd like to go downriver. If oceans exist in Belyyreka, you should have the chance to see one."

The great turtle nodded, and turned, and began swimming along with the river. The current made it easier than it would have been otherwise, and they made good time, Nadya looking all around them as they traveled, making quiet note of the shape of the land. They had hours yet before the sky would darken and they would need to go back through the forest to their own river. Perhaps there were still people here. Perhaps they could be the scouts who rediscovered a city, who reunited a people. Perhaps they would find the oysters after all. She wasn't sure what an oyster tasted like, but she was quite sure that the taste was something worth having, if people still missed it all these years after the lost city became lost.

Burian swam and the river ran, and Nadya relaxed, content and comfortable, confident enough that they were where they belonged that she nearly fell off the turtle when the giant frog abruptly popped out of the water in front of them.

It was larger than Burian, larger than the largest turtle she had ever seen. It was big enough to eat the world. In her sudden fear, Nadya couldn't imagine that anything larger existed in the entire world: it was just the frog, just the single universal frog, the frog that ate a city, the frog that must have eaten all the other frogs.

Burian whirled in the water, beginning to swim frantically back upriver, as Nadya craned her neck to stare. It wasn't the same frog. It couldn't be. It was too large, and even the passage of time wouldn't explain this much increase in size. It was terrible and immense, but it couldn't be the same frog.

The frog's throat inflated. A deep, terrible croaking sound rolled over them, loud enough to hurt Nadya's ears.

Then its tongue lashed out, and caught the back of Burian's shell, yanking the turtle backward. Yanking Nadya backward with him. Burian yelled. Nadya shrieked. The frog continued to pull. They were going to be consumed. They were going to end.

Nadya looked frantically around. The River Winsome had no reason to care about her, or what happened to her, but most of the water near them had to still be rainwater, fresh-fallen and not yet truly a part of this river. It was a stranger here, like she was, and home in the Wild, some of the rainwater had come to her aid when she needed it most. She thrust her right hand into the river, fingers spread, and grabbed the water like it was something she could hold.

When she pulled her hand out of the river, the water *was* something she could hold. Nadya drew forth a glistening sword of water, translucent and sharp, and swung it at the frog's tongue as hard as she could. She had no technique. She had no training. She had strength enough to bring that sword down like a cleaver, slicing through the frog's tongue.

Burian lurched forward, his frantic paddling suddenly of use again, and swam for the bank as hard as he could, orienting himself by the tree line. The frog dove beneath the river, and Nadya saw the great shadow of its body pass beneath them, dark and terrifying.

"Burian, *turn!*" she shouted.

Not fast enough. The frog, injured and angry, surfaced below them, fast enough to knock Nadya from her place on Burian's back. She flailed around, grabbing hold of the lip of skin surrounding the frog's ear. Burian was swimming, not yet swallowed.

"Go! *Go!*" she yelled, and stabbed her water sword into the frog's earhole.

It didn't shriek. It didn't croak. It hissed, flailing in sudden agony, flinging Nadya into the line of white water that marked the boundary between the Winsome and the Wicked. She clawed for the surface, trying to catch her breath against the sudden deluge of heavy water. When her head broke the surface, she saw the frog sinking, twitching but no longer moving, and Burian swimming away from it.

"Buri—" she began, and stopped as water filled her mouth. She continued to thrash, to no avail.

The water pulled her under, and all she knew was darkness.

Her last thought before even thought went away was that a border was very much like a threshold, and a threshold implied the presence of a door.

13 THE EDGE OF THE POND

HANDS GRIPPED HER SHOULDERS and yanked her back into the air. Nadya hung limp, barely aware, as she was laid down on a surface of hard-packed mud. "—she's breathing," said a voice, unfamiliar, strangely accented, with none of the gentle slopes she had come to understand in the city beneath the River Wild.

Perhaps she had found the other city's survivors after all? A hand pressed down on her chest and water bubbled up her throat, filling her mouth. She rolled to the side, vomiting it out, and opened her eyes at the same time, looking down.

She was sprawled on some kind of bank, not on a city dock as she would have expected. Two strangers stood nearby, oddly dressed in blue trousers and thin printed tops, no embroidery, no texture. They were watching her with concern.

"Are you all right, little girl?" one of them asked.

"I've seen her around the neighborhood," said the other. "She's that little Russian orphan Carl and Pansy adopted."

Nadya choked up more water and looked down at herself, horrified but somehow not surprised to see her body as it had looked when she was ten going on eleven, and not as it had looked when she rose from her bed that morning, a woman grown and ready to ride out for the service of her city, river, and home.

Her water arm was gone, replaced by the absence that had

been familiar for so very long, but was now only an aching confirmation of what had happened.

Nadya pushed her feet back under herself and braced her left hand against the mud, levering her body into a standing position. Everything about the motion felt odd. She was too small, too light; there was nothing to her.

The people who had pulled her out of the turtle pond watched her silently, concern in their faces.

"What . . ." she began. "What happened?"

"I saw you floating in the water, facedown, and pulled you out," said the first stranger. "You would have drowned if I hadn't come along when I did."

Nadya looked frantically around. Nothing she could see looked even remotely like a door. The pattern of weed and shadow had been hopelessly disrupted by her fall, the fence was the wrong angle, nothing was right . . .

Nothing was right.

Her prosthetic arm wasn't floating in the pond, and Belyyreka was still a memory, bright and burning, not fading like a dream. She knew who she was. She knew where she belonged. She turned to run, and stopped as one of the people grabbed the back of her jacket, pulling her to a halt.

"Stay here, little miss, while we call your parents and get you seen to," he said.

Nadya didn't struggle.

She no longer remembered the way home from the edge of the water, after all.